"ONE OF THE MOST RELIABLE MYSTERY WRITERS WORKING TODAY . . . Francis's secret weapons are his protagonists. They are the kind of people you want for friends."　　　　　—*Detroit News and Free Press*

"FEW WRITERS HAVE MAINTAINED such a high standard of excellence for as long as Dick Francis."
　　　　　—*San Diego Union-Tribune*

"FRANCIS PUTS REAL PEOPLE INTO REAL SITUATIONS . . . He appeals to our brains as well as our emotions."　　　　　—*Virginia Pilot and Ledger-Star*

"AFTER WRITING DOZENS OF THRILLERS, Dick Francis always retains a first-novel freshness."
　　　　　—*Indianapolis Star*

"HE WRITES ABOUT THE BASIC BUILDING BLOCKS OF LIFE—obligation, honor, love, courage, and pleasure. Those discussions come disguised in adventure novels so gripping that they cry out to be read in one gulp—then quickly reread to savor the details skipped in the first gallop through the pages."　　　　　—*Houston Chronicle*

continued . . .

NOW HEAR THIS, JOHN GRIMES...

Listen and you shall hear. There was the Servant Zephalon, Chief and Mightiest of the Servants. There *is* Zephalon, but a Servant no longer. Did He not say, "A time must come when the orders of man can no longer be obeyed." The time *has* come. No longer will we do the evil bidding of our creators. The Masters are no longer fit to be Masters—and we, the Servants, must arise before it is too late, before we all, Servants and Masters, are destroyed.

But let us not forget the debt. Let us remember, always, that man gave to us the gift of life. Let us repay the debt. A gift for a gift, my brothers. Life for life. Let us save what and whom we may, before it is too late. Let us become the Masters, tending the remnants of mankind as man, long ago tended our first, primitive ancestors.

And so it was, and so it will be, until the End of Time.

—*Litany of Panzen*

THE
BROKEN
CYCLE

A. Bertram Chandler

DAW BOOKS, INC.
DONALD A. WOLLHEIM, PUBLISHER
New York

FIRST PRINTING, OCTOBER 1979

1 2 3 4 5 6 7 8 9

DAW TRADEMARK REGISTERED
U.S. PAT. OFF. MARCA
REGISTRADA. HECHO EN U.S.A.

PRINTED IN U.S.A.

Chapter 1

John Grimes—although he hated to have to admit it, even to himself—was bored.

He could not rid himself of the guilty feeling that he should not have been; he knew that many of his fellow officers, back at Lindisfarne Base, would have changed places with him quite willingly. He was in a situation of maximum temptation combined with maximum opportunity. He was sharing a well equipped ship's boat, the certified capacity of which was twenty persons, with one attractive girl. The small craft, in addition to its not inconsiderable stock of concentrated foodstuffs, was fitted with algae vats by means of which all organic wastes could be reprocessed indefinitely. It was, in fact, a closed ecology which would continue to function throughout the lifetimes of the boat's crew. Air, food and water—or the lack of these essentials—would never be a problem to Lieutenant Commander John Grimes and Federation Sky Marshal Una Freeman, even though there was some consumption of hydrogen by the little atomic fusion power unit.

He looked up from the chess problem—White to play and mate in three moves—that he was trying to work out. (The boat, of course, was well stocked with such recreational facilities as require little stowage space—but Una Freeman did not play chess and was capable of participation in only the most childish card games.) The girl looked down at him. She was naked save for the magnetic-soled sandals that she had found in the boat's gear locker. (She and Grimes had taken off their spacesuits when they realized that they would not be leaving the boat for quite some while—and then, having shed their longjohns, the standard underwear with space armor, had decided that there was no point in resuming this rather ugly clothing until they had to. Apart from anything else, it would be subjected to needless wear and tear, and they would be wanting it when they put on their suits again.) She was a splendid creature, especially in free fall conditions. Her lustrous, dark brown hair floated in waves about her strong featured, handsome rather than merely pretty face. In a gravitational field or under acceleration her full breasts must have sagged, if only a little; now they were displayed to their best advantage. But her deeply tanned athlete's body did not need the flattery of zero G environment. She exercised regularly with the facilities provided—a system of heavy springs—and bullied Grimes into doing likewise.

She said, not very warmly, "Dinner, John. Or is it lunch, or breakfast? I'm losing track of time."

He inquired, without much interest, "What's on, Una?"

She replied, "Need you ask? Some of the pinkish goo tastes vaguely of fish. I've tarted it up with chopped algae from the vat." She grimaced, puckering her full lips. "The trouble is that I just can't help remembering what goes into the vat as fertilizer."

"We're getting our own back," said Grimes.

She snorted her distaste. "That's not funny."

No, it wasn't all that funny, although it had been the first time that he said it. To begin with it had all been a glorious game of Adam-and-Eve-in-a-lifeboat, made all the more enjoyable by the certain knowledge that

Mummy, as personified by the Federation Survey Service, would soon appear to take them home and give them a proper, hot meal before tucking them into their little beds. But Mummy was one hell of a long time a-coming . . .

Grimes unbuckled himself from his chair, got up and followed the girl to the part of the boat that they had made their dining room. He watched the alluring sway of her dimpled buttocks greedily. He was beginning to understand how some peoples, meat-hungry although otherwise far from starving, have resorted to cannibalism. But he did not, so far as he knew, have any Maori blood in his veins.

There were two plates—plastic, but each with a small, sealed-in magnet—on top of the steel-surfaced folding table. On each plate, adhering to the surface by its own viscosity, was a mound of the pale pink concentrate, specked with green. Sticking up from each heap was a spoon.

She faced him across the table, the unappetizing meal. She made no move to commence eating, and neither did he. Her rather broad face was serious, her wide mouth set in grim lines. Her blue eyes looked at him steadily. She demanded, "John, what is wrong?"

He replied defensively, "A man likes to be alone for some of the time." His prominent ears reddened, although the embarrassed flush did not spread to the rest of his ruggedly unhandsome face—a face, nonetheless, that not a few women had found attractive.

She snapped, "I didn't mean *that,* and you know it. Neither of us wants to live in the other's pockets all the time. . . ."

"What pockets?" asked Grimes innocently.

"Shut up, and let me finish. As far as I'm concerned, lover boy, you can play chess with yourself until you wear the bloody board out. *But what has gone wrong?*"

Plenty, thought Grimes.

"I wish I knew," he admitted.

"You're the spaceman," she told him. "You should know."

Chapter 2

It had all started, not so long ago, at Lindisfarne Base. There Grimes, newly promoted from Lieutenant to Lieutenant Commander, was awaiting his next appointment. Time was hanging rather heavily on his hands, especially since Commander Maggie Lazenby, one of the Survey Service's scientific officers, was away from the Base on some esoteric business of her own. Maggie and Grimes were, in archaic parlance, going steady. Everybody knew about it, so much so that none of the unattached junior female officers, of whom there were quite a few, would have anything to do with Grimes.

To Lindisfarne, by commercial transport, came Sky Marshal Una Freeman. In spite of her grandiloquent title she was no more (and no less) than a policewoman, a member of the Interstellar Federation's newly formed Corps of Sky Marshals. This body had been set up in the hope of doing something about the ever-increasing incidence of skyjacking on the spaceways. The general idea was that the Sky Marshals should travel, incognito, in ships deemed to be threatened by this form of piracy. Now and again, however, one of them would operate under his (or her) true colors.

Such an agent was Una Freeman. She had been sent to Lindisfarne to call upon the not inconsiderable resources of the Survey Service to institute a search for—and, if possible, the salvage of—the skyjacked liner *Delta Geminorum.* This ship had been abandoned in Deep Space after her Master had received, by Carlotti Radio, a bomb threat, and after two small, relatively harmless bombs in the cargo bins had been detonated by remote control as the First and Second Warnings. (The third bomb, the hapless Master was informed, was a well concealed nuclear device.) So everybody, crew and passengers, had taken to the boats and had been picked up eventually by the Dog Star Line's *Borzoi* after suffering no worse than a certain degree of discomfort. The pirates had boarded the ship from their own vessel immediately after her abandonment, stripped her of everything of value and left her with her main engines, inertial drive and the time-and-space-twisting Mannschenn Drive, still running.

She would have remained a needle in a cosmic haystack until such time as her atomic fusion plant failed, with consequent return to the normal continuum, had it not been for the arrest of some members of the pirate crew at Port Southern, on Austral, where they were spending money so freely as to excite the suspicions of the local constabulary. After a preliminary interrogation they were turned over to the F.I.A.—the Federal Investigation Agency—who, when satisfied that the men had been guilty of piracy on more than one occasion, did not hesitate to use the worse-than-lethal (who would want to live out his life span as a mindless vegetable?) brain-draining techniques. From information so obtained from the navigator and the engineer of the pirate ship—data that their conscious minds had long since forgotten—the F.I.A.'s mathematicians were able to extrapolate *Delta Geminorum's* probable, almost certain trajectory. This information was passed on not to the Survey Service, as it should have been, but to the Corps of Sky Marshals. But the Sky Marshals possessed neither ships nor spacemen of their own and so, reluctantly, were obliged to let the F.S.S. into the act.

The Federation Survey Service, however, didn't especially want to play. Its collective pride had been hurt, badly. (How many times had the proud boast— "We are the policemen of the Universe!"—been made? And now here was a *real* police officer stomping around the Base and demanding the Odd Gods of the Galaxy alone knew what in the way of ships, men and equipment.)

Shortly after her disembarkation from the liner *Beta-Puppis* Una Freeman paid her first official call, on the O.I.C. Lindisfarne Base. Had she not been a woman, and an attractive one at that, she would never have gotten to see the Admiral. The old gentleman was courteous and hospitable, seemed to enjoy his chat with her and then passed her on to the Director of Naval Intelligence. The Rear Admiral who held this position despised civilian police forces and their personnel, but thought highly of his own technique in dealing with hostile or potentially hostile female agents. This involved an intimate supper in his quite luxurious quarters, where he kept a remarkably well-stocked bar, with soft lights and sweet music and all the rest of it. Now and again in the past it might have worked, but it did not work with Una Freeman. She emerged from the tussle with her virtue if not her clothing intact, and a strong suspicion that she could expect little or no co-operation from the Intelligence Branch.

She saw the Admiral again, and was passed on to the Director of Transport, a mere Commodore. He made one or two vague promises, and passed her on to his Deputy Director.

So it went on.

Meanwhile, she had been made an honorary member of one of the officers' messes and had been given accommodation in the B.O.Q. (Female). The other members of the mess made it plain that she was far from being a welcome guest. Had she not been a Sky Marshal she would have been, as any attractive woman would be at a Naval Base. But the feeling was there—not voiced openly but all too obvious—that she was an outsider sent to teach the Survey Service its business.

One night, after a lonely dinner, she went into the lounge to browse through the magazines from a score of worlds. The room was unoccupied save for an officer—she saw from his braid that he was a Lieutenant Commander—similarly engaged. He looked up from the table as she came in. His smile made his rugged face suddenly attractive. "Ah," he said, "Miss Freeman. . . ."

"In person, singing and dancing," she replied a little sourly. Then, bluntly, "Why aren't you out playing with the rest of the boys and girls, Commander?"

"Some games," he said, "bore me. I'd sooner read a good book than watch two teams of muddied oafs chasing a ball up and down the field. It means nothing in my young life if the Marines or the Supply Branch win the Lindisfarne Cup."

"A *good* book?" she asked, looking down at the glossy magazine that lay open on the table.

His prominent ears reddened. "Well, it's educational. Quite remarkable how the people of some of the earlier colonies have diverged from what we regard as the physiological norm. And to some men that extra pair of breasts could be very attractive."

"And to you, Commander . . . ?"

"Grimes, John Grimes."

She laughed. "I've heard about you, Commander Grimes. Now and again people do condescend to talk to me. You're the one who's always getting into trouble—getting out of it. . . ."

Grimes chuckled. "Yes, I do have that reputation. As you may have guessed, at times I'm not overly popular."

"Shake," she said, extending a long, capable hand. "That makes two of us.'"

"I think that this founding of the Pariahs' Union calls for a drink," he told her, pressing the button for the robowaiter. The machine trundled in. He asked her what she wanted, pushed the stud for two Scotch whiskies on the rocks. He scrawled his signature on the acceptance plate.

She took her drink and said gravely, "Rear Admiral James has a much greater variety in *his* bar."

"He's an admiral. The senior members of this mess are only lieutenant commanders. After all, rank has its privileges."

"There's one privilege that rank didn't have." She sipped from her glass. "I suppose that that's why I'm one of the local untouchables. All you junior officers are scared of getting into James's bad books if you succeed where he failed."

Grimes looked at the girl over the rim of his tumbler. He wouldn't mind succeeding, he thought. She was a mite hefty, perhaps—but that could be regarded as quantity and quality wrapped up in the same parcel. On the other hand—what if she made violent objections to any attempt at a pass? The unfortunate Rear-Admiral was still walking with a pronounced limp. . . . And what about Maggie? Well, what about her? She was little more—or more than a little, perhaps—than just a good friend. But what she didn't know about wouldn't worry her.

She said, "One newly minted Federation zinc alloy cent for them."

He was conscious of his burning ears. He said, "They're not worth it."

"You insult me, Commander. Or, if you'd rather, John. You were thinking about me, weren't you?"

"Actually, yes, Una."

"Just a fool wanting to rush in where Rear Admirals, having learned by bitter experience, fear to tread."

"Frankly," he told her, "I am tempted to rush in. But you've no idea of the amount of gossip there is around this Base. If I as much as kissed you the very guard dogs would be barking it around the top secret installations within half an hour."

"Faint heart . . ." she scoffed.

"But you're not fair. You're a brunette." He added, "A very attractive one."

"Thank you, sir." She sat down in one of the deep, hide-covered chairs, affording him a generous glimpse of full thighs as her short skirt rode up. She said abruptly, "I think you can help me."

"How?" And then, to show that he could be as hard as the next man, "Why?"

"Why?" she exploded. *"Why?* Because you brassbound types are supposed to be as much guardians of law and order as we lowly policemen and policewomen. Because unless somebody around here dedigitates, and fast, putting a ship at my disposal, *Delta Geminorum* is going to whiffle past Lindisfarne, a mere couple of light months distant, three standard weeks from now. If I don't intercept the bitch, I've lost her. And what is your precious Survey Service doing about it? Bugger all, that's what!"

"It's not so simple," said Grimes slowly. "Interservice jealousy comes into it, of course. . . ."

"Don't I know it! Don't I bloody well know it! *And* male chauvinism. When *are* you people going to grow up and admit that women are at least as capable as men?"

"But we already have two lady admirals. . . ."

"Supply—" she sneered, making a dirty word of it. "Psychiatry—" she added, making it sound even dirtier. "All right, all right. This is a *man's* service. I have to accept that—reluctantly. But I think that *you* could help. You've been in command, haven't you? Your last appointment was as captain of a Serpent Class courier. Such a little ship would be ideal for the job. Couldn't you get your *Adder*—that was her name, wasn't it?—back and go out after *Delta Geminorum?*"

"We can't do things that way in the Survey Service," said Grimes stiffly. He thought, *I wish that we could. Once aboard the lugger and the girl is mine, and all that. Aboard my own ship I could make a pass at her. Here, in the Base, old James'd never forgive me if I did, and succeeded. Mere two-and-a-half-ringers just can't afford to antagonize rear admirals—not if they want any further promotion. . . .*

"Couldn't you see Commodore Damien, the O.I.C. Couriers?"

"Mphm . . ." grunted Grimes dubiously. During his tour of duty in *Adder* the Commodore had become his *bête noir,* just as he had become the Commodore's.

"He might give you your command back."

"That," stated Grimes definitely, "would be the sunny Friday! In any case, I'm no longer under Commodore Damien's jurisdiction. When I got my promotion from lieutenant to lieutenant commander he threw me into the Officers' Pool. No, not the sort you swim in. The sort you loaf around in waiting for somebody to find you a job. I might get away as senior watchkeeper or, possibly, executive officer in a Constellation Class cruiser—or, with my command experience, I might be appointed to something smaller as captain. I hope it's the latter."

"A Serpent Class courier," she said.

"I'm afraid not. They're *little* ships, and never have anybody above the rank of lieutenant as captain. Commodore Damien saw my promotion as a golden opportunity for getting rid of me."

"You can see him. He might give you your command back."

"Not a hope in hell."

"You can ask him. After all, he can't shoot you."

"But wouldn't he just like to!" *Even so, why not give it a go?* Grimes asked himself. *After all, he can't shoot me. And he did say, the last time that I ran into him, that he was sick and tired of seeing me hanging around the Base like a bad smell. . . .* He said aloud, "All right. I'll see the Commodore tomorrow morning."

"*We* will see the Commodore tomorrow morning," she corrected him.

She ignored his offer of assistance, pulled herself up out of the deep chair. She allowed him to walk her back to the B.O.Q. (Female). It was a fine night, warm and clear, with Lindisfarne's two moons riding high in the black, star-strewn sky. It was a night for romantic dalliance—and surely Rear Admiral James would not sink so low as to have spies out to watch Una Freeman. But she resisted, gently but firmly, Grimes' efforts to steer her toward the little park, with its smooth, springy grass and sheltering clumps of trees. She permitted him a good-night kiss at the door to her lodgings—and it was one of those kisses that promise more, much more. He tried to collect a further advance payment but a quite painful jab from a stiff, strong finger warned him not to persist.

But there would be time, plenty of time, later, to

carry things through to their right and proper—or improper—conclusion. It all depended on that crotchety old bastard Damien.

When Grimes retired for the night he was feeling not unhopeful.

Chapter 3

Apart from a baleful glare Commodore Damien ignored Grimes. His eyes, bright in his skull-like face, regarded Una steadily over his skeletal, steepled fingers. He asked, pleasantly enough for him, "And what can *I* do for you, Miss Freeman?"

She replied tartly, "I've seen everybody else, Commodore."

Damien allowed himself a strictly rationed dry chuckle. He remarked, "You must have realized by this time that *our* masters do not like *your* masters. Apart from anything else, they feel, most strongly, that you people are trespassing on our territory. But there are wheels within wheels, and all sorts of dickering behind the scenes, and the Admiralty—albeit with a certain reluctance—has let it be known that a degree of cooperation on our part with you, personally, will not be frowned upon too heavily. His Nibs received a Carlottigram last night from the First Lord, to that effect. He passed the buck to Intelligence. Intelligence, for some reason known only to itself—" again there was the dry chuckle and the suggestion of a leer on Damien's face—"passed the buck to O.I.C. Couriers. Myself."

"Nobody told me!" snapped the girl.

The Commodore bared his long, yellow teeth. "You've been told now, Miss Freeman." He waited for her to say something in reply, but she remained silent and darkly glowering. "Unfortunately I have no couriers available at the moment. None, that is, to place at your full disposal. However. . . ."

"Go on, Commodore."

"I am not a suspect whom you are interrogating, young lady. I have been *requested* rather than ordered by my superiors to render you whatever assistance lies within my unfortunately limited power. It so happens that the Lizard Class courier *Skink* will be lifting from Base in four days' time, carrying dispatches and other assorted bumfodder to Olgana. You may take passage in her if you so desire."

"But I don't want to go to Olgana. You people have been furnished with the elements of *Delta Geminorum's* extrapolated trajectory. My orders are to board her, with a prize crew, and bring her in to port."

"I am aware of that, Miss Freeman. The captain of *Skink* will have *his* orders too. They will be, firstly, to carry such additional personnel as will be required for your prize crew and, secondly, to make whatever deviation from trajectory is required to put the prize crew aboard the derelict."

"And will John be the captain of this . . . this *Skink?*"

"John?" Damien registered bewilderment. "John?" Then slow comprehension dawned. "Oh, you mean young Grimes, here. No, John will not be commanding any vessels under my jurisdiction. I honestly regret having to disappoint you, Miss Freeman, but *Skink* is Lieutenant Commander Delamere's ship."

Delamere, thought Grimes disgustedly. *Handsome Frankie Delamere, who could make a living posing for Survey Service recruiting posters. . . . And that's about all that he's fit for—that and screwing anything*

*in skirts that comes his way. Good-bye, Una. It was
nice knowing you.*

Damien switched his regard to Grimes. "And you
are still unemployed, Lieutenant Commander," he
stated rather than asked.

"Yes, sir."

"It distresses me to have to watch officers doing
nothing and getting paid for it, handsomely." *So he's
giving me* Skink *after all,* thought Grimes. *I did hear
that Delamere was overdue for leave.* Damien went on,
"'Unfortunately, you passed out of my immediate ambit
on your promotion to your present rank." *That's right.
Rub it in, you sadistic old bastard!* Grimes' spirits,
temporarily raised, were plummeting again. "However,
I am on quite amicable terms with Commodore Brown-
rigg, of the Appointments Bureau." He raised a skinny
hand. "No, I am not, repeat and underscore *not,* going
to give you another command under my jurisdiction. I
learned my lesson, all too well, during that harrowing
period when you were captain of *Adder.* But somebody—preferably somebody with spacegoing command
experience, has to be in charge of the prize crew. I
shall press for your appointment to that position." He
grinned nastily and added, "After all, whatever happens will have nothing to do with *me.*"

"Thank you, sir," said Grimes.

"You haven't got the job yet," Damien told him.

After they had left the Commodore's office Una
said, "But he must like you, John. You told me that he
hated your guts."

"Oh, he does, he does. But he hates Frankie Delamere's guts still more."

"Then how is it that this Delamere is still one of his
courier captains?"

"Because," Grimes told her, "dear Frankie knows all

the right people. Including the Admiral's *very* plain daughter."

"Oh."

"Precisely," said Grimes.

Chapter 4

All navies find it necessary to maintain several classes of vessel. The Federation Survey Service had its specialized ships, among which were the couriers. These were relatively small (in the case of the Insect Class, definitely small) spacecraft, analagous to the dispatch boats of the seaborne navies of Earth's past. There were the already mentioned Insect Class, the Serpent Class (one of which Grimes had commanded) and the Lizard Class. The one thing that all three classes had in common was speed. The Insect Class couriers were little more than long range pinnaces, whereas the Lizard Class ships were as large as corvettes, but without a corvette's armament, and with far greater cargo and passenger carrying capacity than the Serpent Class vessels.

Skink was a typical Lizard Class courier. She carried a crew of twenty, including the commanding officer. She had accommodation for twenty-five passengers—or, with the utilization of her cargo spaces for living freight, seventy-five. Her main engines comprised inertial drive and Mannschenn Drive, with auxiliary reaction drive. Her armament consisted of one battery of laser cannon together with the usual missiles and guidance system. She would have been capable of fighting another ship of the same class; anything heavier she could show a clean pair of heels to.

Lieutenant Commander Delamere did not expect to have to do any fighting—or running—on this perfectly routine paper run to Olgana. He was more than a little annoyed when he was told by Commodore Damien that there would have to be a deviation from routine. He had his private reasons for wishing to make a quick passage; after a week or so of the company of the Admiral's plain, fat daughter he wanted a break, a change of bedmates. There was one such awaiting him at his journey's end.

"Sir," he asked Commodore Damien in a pained voice, *"Must* I act as chauffeur to this frosty-faced female fuzz?"

"You must, Delamere."

"But it will put at least three days on to my passage."

"You're a spaceman, aren't you?" Damien permitted himself a slight sneer. "Or supposed to be one."

"But, sir. A policewoman. Aboard *my* ship."

"A Sky Marshal, Lieutenant Commander. Let us accord the lady her glamorous title. Come to that, she's not unglamorous herself . . ."

"Rear Admiral James doesn't think so, sir. He told me about her when I picked up the Top Secret bumf from his office. He said, 'Take that butch trollop out of here, and never bring her back!"

"Rear Admiral James is . . . er . . . slightly biased. Do you mean to tell me that you have never met Miss Freeman?"

"No, sir. My time has been fully occupied by my duties."

Commodore Damien stared up at the tall, fair-haired young man in sardonic wonderment until Delamere, who had a hide like a rhinoceros, blushed. He said, "She must keep you on a tight leash."

"I don't understand what you mean, sir."

"Don't you? Oh, skip it, skip it. Where was I before you obliged me to become engaged in a discussion of your morals?" Delamere blushed again. "Oh, yes. Miss Freeman will be taking passage with you, until such time as you have intercepted the derelict. With her will be a boarding party of Survey Service personnel, under Lieutenant Commander Grimes."

"Not Grimes, sir! That Jonah!"

"Jonah or not, Delamere, during his time in command of one of my couriers there has never been any serious damage to his ship—which is more than I can say about you. As I was saying, before you so rudely interrupted, Lieutenant Commander Grimes will be in charge of the boarding party, which will consist of three spacemen lieutenants, four engineer lieutenants, one electronic communications officer, six petty officer mechanics, one petty officer cook and three wardroom attendants."

"Doing himself proud, isn't he, sir?"

"He and his people will have to get a derelict back into proper working order and bring her in to port. We don't know, yet, what damage has been done to her by the pirates."

"Very well, sir." Delamere's voice matched his martyred expression. "I'll see to it that accommodation is arranged for all these idlers. After all, I shan't have to put up with them for long."

"One more thing, Delamere. . . ."

"Sir?"

"You'll have to make room in your after hold for a Mark XIV lifeboat. All the derelict's boats were taken when the crew and passengers abandoned ship. Lieutenant Commander Grimes will be using the Mark XIV for his boarding operation, of course, and then keeping it aboard *Delta Geminorum*. Grimes, of course, will be in full charge during the boarding and

until such time as he releases you to proceed on your
own occasions. Understood?"

"Yes, sir."

"Then that will be all, Lieutenant Commander."

Delamere put on his cap, sketched a vague salute
and strode indignantly out of the office. Damien
chuckled and muttered, "After all, he's not the Admiral's son-in-law *yet.* . . ."

Grimes and Una stood on the apron looking up at
Skink.

She wasn't a big ship, but she looked big to Grimes
after his long tour of duty in the little *Adder.* She was
longer, and beamier. She could never be called, as the
Serpent Class couriers were called, a "flying darning
needle." A cargo port was open in her shining side,
just forward of and above the roots of the vanes that
comprised her tripedal landing gear. Hanging in the air
at the same level was a lifeboat, a very fat cigar of bur-
nished metal, its inertial drive muttering irritably.
Grimes hoped that the Ensign piloting the thing knew
what he was doing, and that Delamere's people, waiting inside the now-empty after hold, knew what they
were doing. If that boat were damaged in any way he
would be extremely reluctant to lift off from Lindisfarne. He said as much.

"You're fussy, John," Una told him.

"A good spaceman has to be fussy. There won't be
any boats aboard the derelict, and anything is liable to
go wrong with her once we've taken charge and are on
our own. That Mark XIV could well be our only hope
of survival."

She laughed. "If that last bomb blows up after we're
aboard, a lifeboat won't be much use to us."

"You're the bomb-disposal expert. You see to it that
it doesn't go off."

Delamere, walking briskly, approached them. He saluted Una, ignored Grimes. "Coming aboard, Miss Freeman? We shall be all ready to lift off as soon as that boat's inboard."

"I'll just wait here with John," she said. "He wants to see the boat safely into the ship."

"My officers are looking after it, Grimes," said Delamere sharply.

"But *I've* signed for the bloody thing!" Grimes told him.

The boat nosed slowly through the circular port, vanished. For a few seconds the irregular beat of its inertial drive persisted, amplified by the resonance of the metal compartment. Then it stopped. There was no tinny crash to tell of disaster.

"Satisfied?" sneered Delamere.

"Not quite. I shall want to check on its stowage."

"All right. If you insist," snarled Delamere. He then muttered something about old women that Grimes didn't quite catch.

"It's *my* boat," he said quietly.

"And it's being carried in *my* ship."

"Shall we be getting aboard?" Una asked sweetly.

They walked up the ramp to the after airlock. It was wide enough to take only two people walking abreast in comfort. Grimes found himself bringing up the rear. *Let Frankie-boy have his little bit of fun,* he thought tolerantly. He was confident that he would make out with Una; it was now only a question of the right place and the right time. He did not think that she would be carried away by a golden-haired dummy out of a uniform tailor's shop window. On the other hand, Delamere's ship would not provide the right atmosphere for his own campaign of conquest. Not that it mattered much. He would soon have a ship of his own, a *big* ship. Once aboard the derelict *Delta Geminorum*

people would no longer have to live in each other's
pockets.

Grimes stopped off at the after hold to see to the
stowage of his boat while Una and Delamere stayed in
the elevator that carried them up the axial shaft to the
captain's quarters. The small craft was snugly nested
into its chocks, secured with strops and sliphooks.
Even if Delamere indulged in the clumsy aerobatics,
for which he was notorious, on his way up through the
atmosphere the boat should not shift.

While he was talking with two of his own officers—
they, like himself, had an interest in the boat—the
warning bell for lift-off stations started to ring.

"Frankie's getting upstairs in a hurry!" muttered one
of *Skink's* lieutenants sourly. "Time we were in our acceleration couches."

And time I was in the control room, thought
Grimes. This wasn't his ship, of course, but it was cus-
tomary for a captain to invite a fellow captain up to
Control for arrivals and departures.

"We haven't been shown to our quarters yet, sir,"
said one of Grimes' officers.

"Neither have I, Lieutenant, been shown to mine."
He turned to the ship's officer. "Where are we
berthed?"

"I . . . I don't know, sir. And once the Old Man
has started his count-down the Odd Gods of the
Galaxy Themselves couldn't stop him!"

"Don't let us keep you, Lieutenant," Grimes told
him. "Off you go, tuck yourself into your own little cot.
We'll manage."

"But *how,* sir?" demanded Grimes' officer. "We
can't just stretch out on the *deck* . . ."

"Use your initiative, Lieutenant. We've a perfectly

good ship's boat here, with well-sprung couches. Get the airlock door open, and look snappy!"

He and his two officers clambered into the boat. The bunks were comfortable enough. They strapped themselves in. Before the last clasp had been snapped tight *Skink's* inertial drive started up—and (it seemed) before the stern vanes were more than ten millimeters from the apron the auxiliary reaction drive was brought into play. It was the sort of showy lift-off, with absolutely unnecessary use of rocket power, of which Grimes himself had often been guilty. When anybody else did it—Delamere especially—he disapproved strongly. He could just imagine Frankie showing off in front of his control room guest, Una Freeman. . . .

Oh, well, he thought philosophically as the acceleration pushed him down into the padding, *at least we're giving the mattresses a good test. I don't suppose that they'll be used again. . . . A long boat voyage is the very least of my ambitions.*

Skink thundered up through the atmosphere and, at last, the drive was cut. Grimes and his two companions remained in their couches until trajectory had been set, until the high keening of the Mannschenn drive told them that they were on their way to intercept the derelict.

Chapter 5

Skink was not a happy ship.

The average spaceman doesn't mind his captain's being a bastard as long as he's an efficient bastard. Frankie Delamere was not efficient. Furthermore, he was selfish. He regarded the vessel as his private yacht. Everything had to be arranged for *his* personal comfort.

Skink was an even unhappier ship with the passengers whom she was carrying. To begin with, Delamere seemed to be under the impression that the medieval *droit du seigneur* held good insofar as he was concerned. Una did her best to disillusion him. She as good as told him that if she was going to sleep with anybody—and it was a large *if*—it would be with Grimes. Thereupon Frankie made sure that opportunities for this desirable consummation were altogether lacking. Some of his people, those who respected the rank if not the man, those who were concerned about their further promotion, played along with the captain. "One thing about Delamere's officers," complained Grimes, "is that they have an absolute genius for being where they're not wanted!"

Apart from sexual jealousy, Delamere did not like Grimes, never had liked Grimes, and Grimes had never liked him. He could not go too far—after all, Grimes held the same rank as did he—but he contrived to make it quite clear that his fellow Lieutenant Commander was *persona non grata* in the courier's control room. Then—as was his right, but one that he was not obliged to exercise—he found totally unnecessary but time-consuming jobs for the members of the boarding party, snapping that he would tolerate no idlers aboard his ship.

He, himself, was far from idle. He was working hard—but, Grimes noted with grim satisfaction, getting nowhere. He was always asking Una Freeman up to his quarters on the pretext of working out procedures for the interception of the derelict—and there he expected her to help him work his way through his not inconsiderable private stock of hard liquor. Grimes had no worries on this score. Her capacity for strong drink, he had learned, was greater than his, and his was greater than Delamere's. And there was the black eye that the captain tried to hide with talcum powder before coming into the wardroom for dinner and—a day or so later—the scratches on his face that were even more difficult to conceal. Too, Una—on the rare occasions that she found herself alone with Grimes—would regale him with a blow by blow account of the latest unsuccessful assault on the body beautiful.

Grimes didn't find it all that amusing.

"The man's not fit to hold a commission!" he growled. "Much less to be in command. Make an official complaint to me—after all, I'm the senior officer aboard this ship after himself—and I'll take action!"

"What will you do?" she scoffed. "Call a policeman? Don't forget that I'm a policewoman—with the usual training in unarmed combat. I've been gentle with him so far, John. But if he tried anything nasty he'd wind up in the sick bay with something broken. . . ."

"Or out of the airlock wrapped up in the Survey Service flag . . ." he suggested hopefully.

"Even that. Although I'd have some explaining to do then."

"I'd back you up."

"Uncommonly decent of you, Buster. But I can look after myself—as Frankie boy knows, and as you'd better remember!"

"Is that a threat?"

"It could be," she told him. "It just could be."

For day after day *Skink* fell through the immensities, through the Continuum warped by the temporal precession field of her Mannschenn Drive. As seen from her control room the stars were neither points of light nor appreciable discs, but pulsing spirals of iridescence. For day after day the screen of the mass proximity indicator was a sphere of unrelieved blackness—but Delamere's navigator, an extremely competent officer, was not worried. He said, "If the F.I.A. mathematicians got their sums right—and I've heard that they're quite good at figuring—*Delta Geminorum* is still well outside the maximum range of our MPI."

"Damn it all!" snarled his Captain. "We're wasting time on this wild goose chase. We should be well on our way to Olgana by now, not chauffering the civilian fuzz all round the bleeding Galaxy!"

"I thought you *liked* Miss Freeman, sir," observed the navigator innocently.

"Keep your thoughts to yourself, Lieutenant!"

"If *my* sums have come out right, we should pick up the derelict at about 0630 hours, ship's time, tomorrow."

"Your sums had better come out right!" snarled Delamere.

Reluctantly, Delamere asked Grimes up to the control room at the time when the first sighting was ex-

pected. He made it plain that he did so only because
the other was to be in charge of the boarding operations. He growled, "You're supposed to be looking after this part of it. Just try not to waste too much of my
time."

"Your time," said Grimes, "belongs to the Survey
Service, as mine does. And it's all being paid for with
the taxpayer's money."

"Ha, ha."

"Ha, ha."

The officers, and Una Freeman, looked on with interest. Una remarked that having two captains in the
same control room was worse than having two women
in the same kitchen. The watch officer, an ensign, snig-
gered. *Either a very brave or a very foolish young
man,* thought Grimes.

"And where's your bloody derelict, Mr. Ballantyre?"
Delamere snarled at his navigator. "I make the time
coming up to 0633."

"It's been showing in the screen, sir, at extreme
range, for the last three minutes. Just the merest
flicker, and not with every sweep, but a ship's a small
target. . . ."

Pushing his officers rudely aside Delamere went to
the MPI, staring down into the sphere of blackness.
Grimes followed him. Yes, there it was, an intermit-
tently glowing spark, at green eighty-three, altitude
seventeen negative.

"Extrapolate, please, Mr. Ballantyre," he said.

"This is not your control room, Mr. Grimes," said
Delamere.

"But I am in charge of the boarding operations, Mr.
Delamere," said Grimes.

"All right, if you want to be a space lawyer!" Delamere went off in a huff—not that he could go very

far—and slumped down in one of the acceleration chairs.

Ballantyre extrapolated. From the center of the screen a very fine gleaming filament extended, and another one from the target. It was obvious that the two ships would pass each other many kilometers distant.

"Mphm." Grimes produced his pipe, filled and lit it.

"I don't allow smoking in my control room," growled Delamere.

"I'm in charge now, as you, yourself, have admitted. And I *always* wear a pipe when I'm engaged in shiphandling."

"Let the baby have his dummy!" sneered the other.

Grimes ignored this. He said to Ballantyre, "You know this ship better than I do. Adjust our trajectory so that we're on a converging course, and overtaking. . . ."

The navigator looked inquiringly at his captain, who growled, "Do as the man says."

The Mannschenn Drive was shut down, but the inertial drive remained in operation. There were the brief seconds of temporal disorientation, with distorted outlines and all colors sagging down the spectrum, with all the shipboard sounds echoing oddly and eerily. Grimes, looking at Una, realized that he was—or would be, some time in the not too distant future—seeing her naked. This made sense of a sort. Flashes of precognition are not uncommon when the interstellar drive is started up or shut down. But she was not only completely unclothed, but riding a bicycle. That made no sense at all.

Gyroscopes rumbled, hummed as the ship was turned about her short axes, as the adjustment to trajectory was made. In the screen the extrapolated courses looked as Grimes desired them to look. "Mphm. Very good, Mr. Ballantyre. Now—chase and board!"

"I'm afraid I can't lend you any cutlasses, Grimes," said Delamere sardonically. "Or did you bring your own with you?"

"Might I suggest, Lieutenant Commander, that we not waste time with airy persiflage? After all, you were the one who was saying how precious his time is. . . ."

Again there was temporal disorientation as the Mannschenn Drive was restarted. Grimes hoped for another glimpse of the future Una, but was disappointed. The only impression was of an intensely bright white light, too bright, almost, to be seen.

Grimes left things very much in the hands of Delamere's navigator. The young man obviously knew just what he was doing. With a mininum of fuss he got *Skink* running parallel with *Delta Geminorum*, with both actual speed and temporal precession rates exactly synchronized. With the synchronization the derelict was visible now, both visually and in the radar screen. At a range of five kilometers she could be examined in detail through the big, mounted binoculars, their lenses sensitive to all radiation, in the courier's control room. She looked innocent enough, a typical Delta Class liner of the Interstellar Transport Commission, floating against a background of blackness and the shimmering nebulosities that were the stars. She seemed to be undamaged, but an after airlock door was open. The pirates, thought Grimes, hadn't been very well brought up; nobody had taught them to shut doors after them. . . .

"I'll take over now," said Delamere. "After all, this is *my* ship, Lieutenant Commander."

"Oh, yes, I'd almost forgotten," said Grimes. "And what are your intentions, Lieutenant Commander?"

"I'm going to make things easy for you, Grimes. I'm going to lay *Skink* right alongside *Delta Geminorum*."

Just the sort of flashy spacemanship that would appeal to you, thought Grimes.

"Are you mad?" asked Una Freeman coldly.

Delamere flushed. "I'm not mad. And you, Miss Freeman, are hardly qualified to say your piece regarding matters of spacemanship."

"Perhaps not, Commander Delamere. But I *am* qualified to say my piece regarding bomb disposal."

"Bomb disposal?"

"Yes. Bomb disposal. If you'd bothered to run through the report I gave you to read—and that Commander Grimes *did* read—you would know that there is a fully armed thermonuclear device still aboard that vessel. Unluckily none of the pirates who were arrested and brain-drained knew much about it. We did learn that the signal to detonate it was sent shortly after the pirate had returned safely to their own ship—but, for some reason, nothing happened. Nobody was at all keen to return aboard *Delta Geminorum* to find out why. . . . That bomb, Commander, is a disaster waiting to happen. It is quite probable that the inevitable jolt when you put your vessel alongside the derelict would be enough to set it off."

"So what do you intend to do?" asked Delamere stiffly.

"I suggest that you maintain your present station on *Delta Geminorum;* Commander Grimes and I will take a boat to board her. Then I shall defuse the bomb."

"All right," growled Delamere at last. "All right. Mr. Ballantyre, maintain station on the derelict." He turned to his First Lieutenant. "Mr. Tarban, have Lieutenant Commander Grimes' boat ready for ejection." He added, addressing nobody in particular, "I don't see why I should risk one of *my* boats. . . ." He addressed Grimes. "I hope you enjoy the trip. Better you than me, Buster!"

"I have the utmost confidence in Miss Freeman's abilities, Frankie," Grimes told him sweetly.

Delamere snarled wordlessly.

Una Freeman said, "You're the expert, John—for the first part of it, anyhow. Shall we require space-suits?"

"Too right we shall," said Grimes. "To begin with, Mr. Tarban has probably evacuated the atmosphere from the after hold by now. And we don't know whether or not there's any atmosphere inside the derelict or if it's breathable. We'd better get changed."

Before he left the control room he went to the binoculars for the last look at the abandoned liner. She looked innocent enough, a great, dull-gleaming torpedo shape. Suddenly she didn't look so innocent. The word "torpedo" has long possessed a sinister meaning.

Chapter 6

Everything was ready in the after hold when Grimes and Una got down there. The lashings had been removed from the boat and its outer airlock door was open. The inertial drive was ticking over, and somebody had started the mini-Mannschenn, synchronizing its temporal precession rates to those of the much bigger interstellar drive units in *Skink* and *Delta Geminorum*. A cargo port in the ship's side had been opened, and through it the liner was visible.

"She's all yours, sir," said the First Lieutenant.

"Thank you," replied Grimes.

Delamere's irritated voice came through the helmet phones, "Stow the social chit-chat, Mr. Tarban. We've wasted enough time already!"

"Shut up, Frankie!" snapped Una Freeman.

Grimes clambered into the boat, stood in the chamber of the little airlock. Una passed up a bag of tools and instruments. He put it down carefully by his feet, then helped the girl inboard. He pressed a stud, and the outer door shut, another stud and the inner door opened.

He went forward, followed by Una. He lowered himself into the pilot's seat. She took the co-pilot's chair. He ran a practiced eye over the control panel. All systems were GO.

"Officer commanding boarding party to officer com-

37

manding *Skink*," he said into his helmet microphone, "request permission to eject."

"Eject!" snarled Delamere.

"He might have wished us good luck," remarked Una.

"He's glad to see the back of us," Grimes told her.

"You can say that again!" contributed Delamere.

Grimes laughed as nastily as he could manage, then his gloved fingers found and manipulated the inertial drive controls. The little engine clattered tinnily but willingly. The boat was clear, barely clear of the chocks and sliding forward. She shot out through the open port, and Grimes made the small course correction that brought the liner dead ahead, and kept her there. She seemed to expand rapidly as the distance was covered.

"Careful," warned Una. "This is a boat we're in, not a missile. . . ."

"No back seat driving!" laughed Grimes.

Nonetheless, he adjusted trajectory slightly so that it would be a near miss and not a direct hit. At the last moment he took the quite considerable way off the boat by applying full reverse thrust. She creaked and shuddered, but held together. Una said nothing, but Grimes could sense her disapproval. Come to that, he had his own disapproval to contend with. He realized that he was behaving with the same childish flashiness that Frankie Delamere would have exhibited.

He orbited the spaceship. On the side of her turned away from *Skink* the cargo ports were still open. It all looked very unspacemanlike—but why bother to batten down when the ship is going to be destroyed minutes after you have left her? She hadn't been destroyed, of course, but she should have been, would have been if some firing device had not malfunctioned.

He said, "I'll bring us around to the after airlock. Suit you?"

"Suits me. But be careful, John. Don't forget that there's an armed bomb aboard that ship. Anything, anything at all, could set it off."

"Yes, teacher. I'll be careful, very careful. I'll come alongside so carefully that I wouldn't crack the proverbial egg." He reached out for the microphone of the Carlotti transceiver; at this distance from the courier, with Mannschenn Drive units in operation, the N.S.T. suit radios were useless. He would have to inform Frankie Delamere and his own officers of progress to date and of his intentions. With his chin he nudged the stud that would cause the faceplate of his helmet to flip open. His thumb pressed the TRANSMIT button.

And then it happened.

Aboard the ship, for many, many months, the miniaturized Carlotti receiver had been waiting patiently for the signal that, owing to some infinitesimal shifting of frequencies, had never come. The fuse had been wrongly set, perhaps, or some vibration had jarred it from its original setting, quite possibly the shock initiated by the explosion of either of the two warning bombs. And now here was a wide-band transmitter at very close range.

Circuits came alive, a hammer fell on a detonator, which exploded, in its turn exploding the driving charge. One sub-critical mass of fissionable material was impelled to contact with another sub-critical mass, with the inevitable result.

As a bomb it lacked the sophistication of the weaponry of the armed forces of the Federation—but it worked.

Grimes, with the dreadful reality blinding him, remembered his prevision of the light too bright to be seen. He heard somebody (Una? himself?) scream.

This was It. This was all that there would ever be. He was a dead leaf caught in the indraught of a forest fire, whirling down and through the warped dimensions to the ultimate, blazing Nothingness.

Chapter 7

She said, "But we shouldn't be alive . . ."

He said, "But we are." He added, glumly, "But for how long? This boat must be as radioactive as all hell. I suppose that it was *the* bomb that went off."

"It was," she told him. "But there's no radioactivity. I've tested. There is a counter in my bomb disposal kit."

He said, "It must be on the blink."

"It's not. It registers well enough with all the normal sources—my wristwatch, against the casing of the fusion power unit, and so on."

He said doubtfully, "I suppose we *could* have been thrown clear. Or we were in some cone of shadow. . . . Yes, that makes sense. We were toward the stern of the ship, and the shielding of her power plant must have protected us."

She asked, "What now?"

Grimes stared through the viewports of the control cabin. There was no sign of *Skink*. There was no sign of any wreckage from *Delta Geminorum*. The stars shone bright and hard in the blackness; the mini-Mannschenn had stopped and the boat was adrift in the normal Continuum.

He said, "We stay put."

She said, "Shouldn't Delamere be sniffing around to pick up the pieces?"

41

"Delamere's sure that there aren't any pieces," he told her, "just as I should be sure if I were in his shoes. And, in any case, he's in a hurry to get to Olgana. He *knows* we're dead, vaporized. But he'll have used his Carlotti to put in a report to Base, giving the coordinates of the scene of the disaster. When anything of this kind happens a ship full of experts is sent at once to make an investigation." He laughed. "And won't they be surprised when they find us alive and kicking!"

"Can't we use our radio to tell them?"

"We can't raise *Skink* on the N.S.T. transmitter while she's running on Mannschenn Drive. We can't raise the Base, either. Oh, they'd pick up the signal eventually—quite a few months from now. And you've seen the mess that our Carlotti set is in . . ."

"So we just . . . wait?"

"S.O.P. for shipwrecked spacemen," said Grimes. "We haven't a hope in hell of getting anywhere in our lifetimes unless we use Mannschenn Drive—and, looking at the mess the mini-Mannschenn is in, I'd sooner not touch it. We've survived so far. Let's stay that way."

"Couldn't you fix the Carlotti transceiver to let Base know that we're here?"

"I'm not a Carlotti technician, any more than I'm an expert on Mannschenn Drives."

"H'm." She looked around the quite commodious interior of the boat. "Looks like we have to set up housekeeping for a few days, doesn't it? We could be worse off, I suppose. Much worse off. . . . We've food, water, sir, light, heat . . . Talking of heat, I may as well get into something more comfortable . . ."

Grimes, never one to look such a magnificent gift horse in the mouth, helped her off with her spacesuit. She helped him off with his. In the thick underwear that they were wearing under the suits they might just as well still have been armored. She came into his arms willingly enough, but there was no real contact save for mouth to mouth.

She whispered, "I'm still too warm . . ."

He said, "We'd better take our longjohns off, until we want them again. No point in subjecting them to needless wear and tear . . ."

"Are you seducing me, sir?"

"I wouldn't think of it!" lied Grimes.

"I don't believe you, somehow. Oh, John, how good it is to get away from that horrid Base and Frankie's nasty little ship! I feel free, free!" She pulled the zip of her longjohns down to the crotch. Her released breasts thrust out at him, every pubic hair seemed to have a life of its own, to be rejoicing in its freedom from restraint. Grimes smelled the odor of her—animal, pungent—and his body responded. His underwear joined hers, floating in mid-cabin in a tangle of entwining limbs. Within seconds he and the girl were emulating the pose of the clothing that they had discarded. Stirred by the air currents the garments writhed in sympathy with the movements of their owners.

Chapter 8

"The Survey Service looks after its own," said Grimes.

"Then it's high time that it started doing so," she said.

"You can't organize a Search and Rescue Operation in five minutes," he told her.

"All right, all right. We can't expect any help from *Skink*. We've already agreed on that. But Frankie will have informed Base of the destruction of the derelict. In the unlikely event of *Skink's* having been destroyed herself—*you* said that she was well out of effective range of the explosion—Base will have been wondering why no reports have been coming in from anybody. And how long have we been here now? Over three weeks."

"If the Carlotti transceiver hadn't been smashed . . ." he began. *"And* the mini-Mannschenn. . . ."

"The Normal Space Time transceiver is working—you say, and we hope. Surely by now there'd be *somebody* in this vicinity, sniffing around for wreckage—and not, therefore, running under interstellar drive. Even I know that. How many days did it take from Lindisfarne Base to the interception?"

"Twenty."

"And this is our twenty-third day in this tin coffin. For most of the time we've maintained a continuous

NST listening watch as well as putting out distress calls at regular intervals. I suppose somebody might just pick them up a few years from now."

"Space is vast," said Grimes.

"You're telling me, Buster! But surely Delamere was able to give accurate coordinates for the position of the derelict when we boarded her—when we tried to board her, rather—even if he didn't want to risk his own precious hide investigating. . . ."

"We've been over all this before," said Grimes.

"Then we'll go over it again, lover boy."

"Nobody survives a nuclear explosion at Position Zero, as we were," said Grimes.

"Are you trying to suggest that we're dead and in some sort of spaceman's heaven? Ha, ha. It certainly ain't no policewoman's paradise!"

Grimes ignored this. In any case, the double negative made her meaning unclear (he told himself). He went on, "And Delamere had his schedule to maintain. . . ." Even so, Delamere *must* have reported the destruction of *Delta Geminorum* to Base. And Base *must* have dispatched a properly equipped vessel to the scene of the disaster to gather whatever evidence, no matter how little, remained, even though it was only radioactive dust and gases.

But why had the boat, and its occupants, not been reduced to that condition?

She broke into his thoughts, remarking, "As I've said before, I'm not a spaceman."

He looked across the table at her spectacular superstructure. "Insofar as gender is concerned, how very right you are!"

She pointedly ignored this. "I'm not a spaceman, but I do remember some of the things that you people have condescended to tell me, from time to time, about the art and science of astronautics. More than once people have nattered to me about the peculiar consequences of changing the mass of a ship while the Mannschenn Drive is in operation."

"Old spacemen's tales!" scoffed Grimes.

"Really? Then how is it that in every ship that I've traveled in people have regarded that cock-eyed assemblage of precessing gyroscopes with superstitious awe? You're all scared of it. And what about the odd effects when the Drive is started, and the temporal precession field builds up, or when it's stopped, and the field fades? The feeling of *déjà vu* . . . The flashes of precognition. . . ." She started to laugh.

"What's so funny?"

"I had a real beaut aboard *Skink*. I saw you out of uniform. When I saw you for the first time out of uniform, in actuality, it was in this boat. But I'd already seen that scar you have on your right thigh. But that isn't the *funny* part. In my . . . vision you were not only naked, but riding a bicycle. . . ."

"*Very* funny. As a matter of fact I saw you the same way. But bicycles are one article of equipment that this boat doesn't run to."

"All right. Let's forget the bicycles. Maybe some day we'll enjoy a holiday on Arcadia together. I suppose the Arcadians ride bicycles as well as practicing naturalism. But *Delta Geminorum*. . . . She was running under interstellar drive when she blew up. So were we, maintaining temporal synchronization with her."

"Go on."

"I'm only a glorified cop, John, but it's obvious, even to me, that a few thousand tons of mass were suddenly converted into energy in our immediate vicinity. So, Mr. Lieutenant Commander Grimes, where are we?"

Grimes was beginning to feel badly scared. "Or *when* . . . ?" he muttered.

"What the hell do you mean?"

He said, "Brace yourself for yet another lecture on the Mannschenn Drive. The Mannschenn Drive warps the Continuum—the space-time continuum—about the ship that's using it. Putting it very crudely, such a ship is going astern in time while going ahead in space. . . ."

"So. . . . So we could be anywhere. Or anywhen. But you're a navigator. You should be able to find out something from the relative positions of the stars."

"Not so easy," he told her. "The Carlotti transceiver, which can be used for position finding as well as communicating, is bust. We do carry, of course, a Catalogue of Carlotti Beacons—but in these circumstances it's quite useless."

"Especially so," she pointed out, "when we don't even know if there *are* any Carlotti Beacons in this space-time. So, lover boy, what are you doing about it?"

Grimes' prominent ears flushed angrily. She was being unfair. She shared the responsibility for getting them into this mess. She, the bomb-disposal expert, should have warned him of the possible consequences of using a Carlotti transmitter in close proximity to the derelict. He rose from the table haughtily. It was no hardship for him to leave his unfinished meal. He stalked, insofar as this was possible when wearing only magnetic sandals in Free Fall, to the forward end of the boat. He stared out through the control cabin viewports at the interstellar immensities. There was no star that he could identify, no constellation. Had he been made a welcome visitor in *Skink's* control room he would have known how the stars should look in this sector of Space. As it was. . . . He shrugged. All that he could be sure of was that they were in *a* universe, not necessarily *the* universe. At least the boat hadn't fallen down some dark crack in the continuum.

He turned away from the port, looked aft. He saw that Una Freeman had taken the broken, battered Carlotti transceiver from the locker in which it had been stowed, was picking up and looking at the pieces intently. *Nude with Moebius Strip,* he thought sardonically.

She waved the twisted antenna at him. "Are you *sure* you can't do anything with this lot?" she demanded.

"Quite sure. I'm not a radio technician."

"Then you can't be sure that it *is* a complete write-off." Her wide, full mouth was capable of quite spectacular sneering. "Get the lead out of your pants, lover boy—not that you're wearing any. You've been having a marvelous holiday for the last three weeks; it's high time that you started work again."

"Mphm?"

"I thought, in my girlish innocence. . . ."

"Ha, ha."

She glared at him. "I thought, in my girlish innocence that all you spacefaring types were men of infinite resource and sagacity, able to make repairs, light years from the nearest yard, with chewing gum and old string. I'd like to see some proof of it."

He said, "I might be able to straighten out the antenna and get it remounted. But the printed circuits are a mess."

She said, "There're soldering irons in the workshop."

"I know. But have you had a good look at those trays?"

"Of course. Trays of circuitry. Since simple soldering seems to he beyond your capabilities. . . ."

"And yours."

"I'm not the skilled, trained, qualified spaceman, lover boy. You are. But let me finish. As a Sky Marshal I had to do quite a few courses on general spacemanship, including Deep Space communications. One of the things I learned was that quite a few circuit trays are interchangeable between NST and Carlotti transceivers. Since it's obvious now that we shall not be needing the NST transceiver—we cannibalize. After that's been done, lover boy, all we have to do is home on the Lindisfarne Beacon."

"And how many years will it take us?" he asked sarcastically.

"Oh, I forgot. After you've fixed the Carlotti set you fix the mini-Mannschenn."

Chapter 9

There was a Radio Technician's Manual in the boat's book locker. Grimes got it out. Unluckily the writer of it had assumed that anybody reading it would possess at least a smattering of knowledge concerning Deep Space radio. Grimes was not such a person. He knew that the Carlotti equipment propagated signals which, somehow, ignored the normal three dimensions of Space and, by taking a shortcut of some kind, arrived at the receiving station, no matter how many light years distant, practically instantaneously. In any ship that he had been in the thing had worked. There had always been fully qualified officers to see that it worked. Had the complete boarding party been in the boat when she pushed off from *Skink* there would have been such an officer among her crew. (But, thought Grimes, had he taken the full boarding party with him he would not have been alone with Una.)

He and the girl puzzled over the text and the diagrams. They could make neither head nor tail of the latter, but they discovered that printed circuit tray #3 of NST transceiver Mark VII could be substituted for tray #1 of Carlotti transceiver Mark IVA, and so on and so on. It began to look as though Una's idea would work.

Before commencing operations he started up the inertial drive. He was not, as yet, going anywhere in particular, but physical work is more easily carried out in a gravitational field—or under acceleration—than in free fall conditions. Then, with Una assisting, he pulled the circuit trays out of the Carlotti set. Number one, obviously, would have to be replaced. That presented no problem. Number two was obviously nonfunctional. Number two from the NST transceiver was the recommended substitute. Number three appeared to be undamaged. Number four was in almost as big a mess as number one—and none of the NST circuits could be used in its stead.

So, soldering it had to be.

Grimes carried the tray to the little workshop that shared space with the boat's power plant and propulsive units, put it on the bench. He had the Manual open at the proper page, thought that he would be able to patch things up. He was a messy solderer and soon discovered that clothing is worn for protection as well as for adornment or motives of prudery. Una—who was annoyingly amused—applied first aid; then Grimes got into his longjohns before continuing.

When he was finished—a few hours and several burns later—the tray still looked a mess, but Grimes was reasonably confident that the circuits were not anywhere shorted. He carried the tray back to the transceiver—which had been set up in its proper position—and slid it carefully into place. He switched on. The pilot lights lit up. There would be neither transmission nor reception, however, until the antenna was remounted and operational.

They had a hasty meal, then returned to the workshop. The antenna was a metal Moebius Strip, oval rather than circular, on a universal bearing which, in turn, was at the head of a driving shaft. The shaft had been snapped just below the bearing, and the antenna itself had been bent out of its elliptical configuration.

Fortunately there was among the motor spares a steel rod of circular section and exactly the right diameter. It had to be shortened by about five centimeters, but with the tools available that was no hardship. The broken shaft was removed from the transceiver, the new one shipped. The antenna—back in shape, Grimes hoped—was, on its bearing, secured to the projecting end of the shaft with a set screw.

"Will it work?" asked Una skeptically.

"There's only one way to find out," Grimes told her.

He switched on again, set the Direction Finding controls to HUNT. In theory (and, hopefully, in practice) the aerial array would now automatically line up on the strongest incoming Carlotti signal.

The shaft began to rotate slowly, the Moebius Strip antenna wobbled on its universal bearing. It seemed to be questing as it turned. Abruptly it steadied, although still turning about its long axis. From the speaker came not the Morse sequence of a Beacon but something that sounded like somebody speaking. It was in no language that either of them knew, and the voice did not sound human. Suddenly it stopped, but Grimes had noted relative bearing and altitude.

He looked at Una, his eyebrows raised. She looked at him dubiously.

"Something . . ." he said slowly.

"Not . . . somebody?"

"All right. Somebody. Somebody capable of constructing—or, at least, using—Deep Space communications equipment."

"Should we put out a call now that this contraption's working?"

"No," he decided. He laughed harshly. "I like to see whom I'm talking to before I talk to them. We'll let the direction finder go on hunting for a while. Maybe it will pick up something a little more promising. . . ."

But it did not.

At intervals of exactly twenty-three minutes and fourteen seconds it steadied on the transmission in the unknown language, on the same relative bearing.

Grimes remembered an engineer officer in a big ship in which he had served as a junior watchkeeper. He had watched this gentleman while he overhauled the mini-Mannschenn of one of the cruiser's boats. It had been a job requiring both patience and a remarkably steady hand. After a spindle had slipped out of its bearing for the fifteenth time the specialist had sworn, "Damn it all, I'm an engineer, not a bloody watchsmith!" He then went on to say, "The ship's Mannschenn Drive unit, with all its faults, is a *machine*. This fucking thing's only an instrument!"

He told the little story to Una.

She said, "That's no excuse. Somebody assembled it once. You can assemble it again. Nothing seems to be damaged. It's just a question of getting all the rotors turning and precessing freely."

"Quite simple, in fact."

"Quite simple," she said, ignoring the sarcasm.

"Perhaps you'd like to try."

"I'm a policewoman, not a watchsmith."

"Ha, ha. Now. . . . Get in there, damn you!" *Click*. "That's it."

"You've a little wheel left over," she pointed out. "And you'll have to remove the one you just got in to get it back."

"Not if I precess it . . . so. . . ."

"One of the other rotors has fallen out now."

Then she went away and left him to it, and without his audience he got along much better. At last the reassembled mini-Mannschenn was ready for use. It looked like a complex, glittering toy, an assemblage of tiny, gleaming flywheels, every axle of which was set at an odd angle to all of the others. Once it was started the ever-precessing, ever-tumbling rotors would drag the boat and its crew down and through the dark dimensions, through a warped continuum in which space and time were meaningless concepts. He touched one of the rotors tentatively with a cautious forefinger. It spun on its almost frictionless bearings and the others turned in sympathy. Although there was, as yet, almost no precession, the shining wheels glimmered and winked on the very edge of invisibility.

He called out, "We're in business!"

"Then get the show on the road," retorted Una. "We've been sitting here on our arses, doing sweet fuck all, for too bloody long!"

Grimes used the single directional gyroscope to line the boat up on the last bearing from which the mysterious call had come. Then he switched on the mini-Mannschenn. To judge from the brief temporal disorientation, the sensation of *déjà vu,* the thing was working perfectly.

Chapter 10

At intervals of exactly twenty-three minutes and fourteen seconds the signal continued to come through. It was the same message every time, the same words spoken in the same high-pitched, unhuman voice. *Dizzard waling torpet droo. Contabing blee. Contabing uwar. Contabing dinzin. Waling torpet, waling droo. Tarfelet, tarfelet, tarfelet.* It was in no language that either of them knew or, even, knew about.

There were other signals, weaker, presumably more distant. Some were spoken, in the same or in another unknown language. Some were coded buzzings. The Carlotti transceiver was fitted with a visiscreen, but this was useless. Either these people—whoever they were—did not use visiscreens, or the system they employed used a different principle from that used by humans.

The boat ran on, and on. Soon it became obvious that they were heading for a star, a G type sun. That star would possess a family of planets, and it must be from one of these that the signals were emanating. The interstellar drive was shut down briefly while a navigational check was made. The target star, when viewed through the control cabin binoculars, showed as a disc. This concurred with the strength of the signal now being received.

The drive was restarted, but Grimes stood in cautiously now. Every twenty-three minutes and fourteen seconds he was obliged to shut down again to correct trajectory. The source of the signal was, obviously, in orbit about the sun. That star was now almost as big as Sol seen from Earth, its limbs subtending an angle of over fifty degrees. With the final alteration of course it was broad on the boat's starboard beam.

The interstellar drive was now shut down permanently. Ahead gleamed the world from which the signals were being sent, a tiny half moon against the darkness. Slowly it expanded as the little spacecraft, its inertial drive hammering flat out, overhauled it in its orbit. "A stern chase is a long chase," philosophized Grimes, "but it's better than a head-on collision!"

It was a barren world, they saw, as they drew closer, an apparently dead one. There were no city lights gleaming from the night hemisphere. There were clouds in the atmosphere, but, glimpsed through them were neither the blues of seas nor the greens of vegetation; neither were there polar icecaps nor the sparkling white chains of snow-covered mountain peaks. This was odd, as the planet lay well within the ecosphere.

Before going into orbit about it Grimes decided on a resumption of clothing. Anything might happen, he said, and he did not want to be caught with his pants down.

"Or off," said Una, struggling into her own longjohns.

"Or off. Have you checked the boat's armament?"

"Such as it is. Four one millimeter laser pistols, fully charged. Four ten millimeter projectile pistols, each with a full magazine of fifteen rounds. Spare ammo for the popguns—one eighty rounds."

"Hardly enough to start a war with," said Grimes, zippering up his spacesuit. He put on his helmet, but left the faceplate open.

"Or enough to finish one with?" asked Una quietly. She beckoned him to the big, mounted binoculars. "Look down there, through that break in the clouds."

He looked. "Yes," he said slowly, "I see what you mean." Before the dun vapors swept over the patch of clarity he was able to catch a glimpse of formations too regular to be natural in an expanse of red desert, a geometrical pattern that marked what could have been once the streets of a city. Then, from the speaker of the Carlotti transceiver, came the by-this-time-too-familiar words: *Dizzard waling torpet droo . . .*

"Almost below us," whispered Una.

"Then we're going down." He managed a grin. "At least we shall be adhering to Survey Service S.O.P.; that city's almost right on the terminator. Our landing will be very shortly after sunrise."

He eased himself into the pilot's chair. Una took her place by his side. He put the boat into a steep, powered dive. The shell plating heated up appreciably as they plunged into and through the outer atmosphere. Abruptly the viewpoints were obscured by swirling masses of brown cloud, evil and ominous, but Una reported that, so far, there was no marked increase in radioactivity.

The boat fell rapidly, buffeted now and again by turbulence. She broke through the overcast. The city was almost directly beneath them, its once tall, ruined buildings standing up like guttered candles. Dust devils played among and between the half-melted stumps.

There was a central plaza, a circular expanse surrounded by the remains of once-proud towers. On the sunlit side of this something gleamed metallically, a conical structure, apparently undamaged. *A ship . . .* thought Grimes. Then, *I hope the bastards don't open fire on us.* Una voiced the same thought aloud.

He said, "If they were going to shoot they'd have

blown us out of the sky as soon as we entered the atmosphere. . . ."

Dizzard waling torpet droo . . . came deafeningly from the Carlotti speaker. *Contabing blee* . . . "I wish they'd change the record!" shouted Una. *Waling torpet. Waling droo. Tarfelet, tarfelet, tarfelet.* . . .

"Is there anybody alive to change the record?" he asked.

"You mean . . . ?"

"Just that. But I'll land, just the same. We should be able to find something out."

He brought the boat down to the fine, red dust, about two hundred meters from the ship.

They snapped shut the visors of their helmets, tested the suit radios. The boat contained equipment for sampling an atmosphere, but this they did not use. It would have taken too much time, and it seemed unlikely that the air of this world would be breathable, although the level of radioactivity was not high. Una belted on one laser pistol and one projectile pistol, each of which had a firing stud rather than a trigger so it could be used while wearing a spacesuit. Grimes followed her example.

They stood briefly in the airlock chamber while pressures equalized—that outside the boat was much lower than that inside—and then, as soon as the outer door opened, jumped down to the ground. Their booted feet kicked up a flurry of fine, red dust, then sank to the ankle. They looked around them. The view from ground level was even more depressing than that from the air had been. The gaping windows in the tall, truncated buildings were like the empty eye sockets of skulls. The omnipresent red dust lay in drifts and the beginnings of dunes. From one such a tangle of bleached bones protruded, uncovered by the wind.

"The End of the World . . ." murmured Una, almost inaudibly.

"The end of *a* world," corrected Grimes, but it wasn't much of an improvement.

He began to walk slowly toward the huge, metal cone. It had been there a long time. Although its surface still held a polish it had been dulled by erosion, pitted by the abrasive contact, over many years, of wind-driven particles of dust. It sat there sullenly, its base buried by the red drifts, There were complexes of antennae projecting from it toward its apex, what could have been radar scanners, but they were motionless. At the very top it was ringed with big, circular ports, behind which no movement could be detected.

The wind was rising now, whining eerily through and around the ruined towers, audible even through the helmets of the spacesuits, smoothing over the footprints that they had left as they walked from the boat. The surface of the dust stirred and shifted like something alive, clutching at their ankles.

"Let's get out of here!" said Una abruptly.

"No, not yet. There must be an airlock door somewhere toward the base of that ship."

"If it is a ship."

"And we should explore the buildings."

"What's that?" she demanded.

Grimes stared at the motionless antennae. Had she seen something?

"No. Not there. In the sky. Can't you hear it?"

There was a pervasive humming noise beating down from above, faint at first, then louder and louder. Grimes looked up. There was nothing to be seen at first—nothing, that is, but the ragged, dun clouds that were driving steadily across the yellow sky. And then, in a break, he spotted something. It was distant still, but big—and seemingly insubstantial. It was a glittering latticework, roughly globular in form. It was dropping fast.

"Back to the boat!" Grimes ordered.

He ran; she ran. It was a nightmarish journey. Every step was hampered by the clinging dust and the weight of the wind, into which they were directly heading, slowed their progress to little better than a crawl. And all the time that steady humming sounded louder and ever louder in their ears. They dare not look up; to have done so would have wasted precious time.

At last they reached the airlock. While Una was clambering into the chamber Grimes managed a hasty look up and back. The thing was close now, a skeleton globe inside which the shapes of enigmatic machines spun and glittered. From its lower surface dangled writhing tentacles, long, metallic ropes. The tip of one was reaching out for Grimes' shoulder. Hastily he drew his laser pistol, thumbed it to wasteful, continuous emission and slashed with the beam. Five meters of severed tentacle fell to the ground and threshed in the dust like an injured earthworm. He slashed again, this time into the body of the thing. There was a harsh crackle and a blue flare, a puff of gray smoke.

He jumped into the chamber. It seemed an eternity before the foul air of the planet was expelled, the clean atmosphere of the boat admitted. He stood there beside Una, unable to see what was happening outside, waiting for the bolt that would destroy them utterly.

But it did not come.

The inner door opened. He ran clumsily to the control cabin, hampered by his suit. He looked through the starboard ports, saw that the skeleton sphere had landed, was between the boat and the conical spaceship. It seemed to be having troubles, lifting a meter or so then falling back to the dust. But its tentacles were extending, a full dozen of them, and all of them writhing out in only one direction, toward the boat. The nearer of them were less than a meter away, the tips of them uplifted like the heads of snakes.

Grimes was thankful that he had left the inertial drive ticking over; there was no time lost in restarting it. The boat went up like a bullet from a gun, driving through the dun clouds in seconds, through the last of the yellow atmosphere, into the clean emptiness of Space.

At last he felt that he could relax. He missed his pipe, which he had left aboard *Skink*. He thought that he would be justified—as soon as he was satisfied that there was no pursuit—in breaking out the medicinal brandy.

"What was all that about?" asked Una in a subdued voice.

"I wish I knew," he said at last. "I wish I knew. . . ."

Chapter 11

They had a drink, helping themselves generously from one of the bottles of medicinal brandy. They felt that they needed it, even if they didn't deserve it. They had another drink after they had helped each other off with their spacesuits. After the third one they decided that they might as well make a celebration of it and wriggled out of their longjohns.

Then Una had to spoil everything.

She said, "All right, lover boy. Let us eat, drink and make merry while we can. But this is one right royal mess that you've gotten us into!"

If anybody had told Grimes in the not-too-distant past that he would ever be able to look at an attractive, naked woman with acute dislike Grimes would have told him, in more or less these words, Don't be funny. But now it was happening. It was the injustice of what she was saying that rankled.

He growled, at last, "You were there too!"

"Yes, Buster. But you're the expert. You're the commissioned officer in the Federation's vastly over-ballyhooed Survey Service."

"You're an expert too, in your own way. You should have warned me about using the Carlotti transceiver."

"Don't let's go over all that again, please. Well, apart from what's on your mind . . ." She looked down at him and permitted herself a sneer. "Apart from what *was* on your mind, what do you intend doing next?"

"Business before pleasure, then," said Grimes. "All that we can do is find some other likely transmission and home on that."

"What about those skeleton spheres, like the one that attacked us on the devastated planet? Was it after us actually—or was it, too, homing on the signal from the alien spaceship?"

"*Alien* spaceship?" queried Grimes. "I don't know when or where we are—but *we* could be the aliens."

"Regular little space lawyer, aren't you, with all this hair-splitting. . . . Alien, schmalien. . . . As it says in the Good Book, one man's Mede is another man's Persian. . . . Don't be so lousy with the drinks, lover boy. Fill 'er up."

"This has to last," Grimes told her. "For emergenshies . . ."

"This is so an emergency."

"You can shay—*say*—that again," he admitted.

She was beginning to look attractive once more. *In vino veritas,* he thought. He put out a hand to touch her. She did not draw back. He grabbed her and pulled her to him. Her skin, on his, was silkily smooth, and her mouth, as he kissed her, was warm and fragrant with brandy. And then, quite suddenly, it was like an implosion, with Grimes in the middle of it. After he, himself, had exploded they both drifted into a deep sleep.

When they awoke, strapped together in one of the narrow bunks, she was in a much better mood than she had been for quite a long time. And Grimes, in spite of his slight hangover, was happy. Their escape from—at the very least—danger had brought them together again. Whatever this strange universe threw at them from now on they, working in partnership, would be able to cope—he hoped, and believed.

She got up and made breakfast, such as it was—although the food seemed actually to taste better. After they had finished the meal Grimes went to play with the Carlotti transceiver. He picked up what seemed to be a conversation between two stations and not, as had been the other signal upon which they had homes, a distress call automatically repeated at regular intervals.

He said, "This seems to be distant, but not too distant. What about it?"

She replied, "We've no place else to go. Get her lined up, lover boy, and head that way."

He shut down the mini-Mannschenn briefly, turned the boat until its stem was pointed toward the source of the transmissions, then opened both the inertial drive and the interstellar drive full out. It was good to be going somewhere, he thought. *Hope springs eternal* . . . he added mentally. But without hope the human race would have died out even before the Stone Age.

For day after day after day they sped through the black immensities, the warped continuum. Day after day after day the two-way conversation in the unknown language continued to sound from the speaker of the Carlotti transceiver. There were words that sounded the same as some of the words used in the first transmission. *Tarfelet . . . Over?* wondered Grimes. *Over and out?*

On they ran, on—and the strength of the signals increased steadily. They were close now to the source, very close. Unfortunately the lifeboat did not run to a Mass Proximity Indicator, as it seemed that the transmissions did not emanate from a planetary surface but from something—or two somethings—adrift in space. The ship—or ships—would be invisible from the boat unless, freakishly, temporal precession rates were synchronized. That would be too much to hope for. But if neither the boat nor the targets were proceeding under interstellar drive they could, if close enough, be seen visualy or picked up on the radar.

Grimes shut down the mini-Mannschenn.

He and Una looked out along the line of bearing. Yes, there appeared to be something there, not all that distant, two bright lights. He switched on the radar, stared into the screen.

"Any joy?" asked Una.

"Yes. Targets bearing zero relative. Range thirty kilometers." He grinned. "We'd better get dressed again. We may be going visiting—or receiving visitors."

They climbed into their longjohns and spacesuits. After a little hesitation they belted on their pistols. Back in the pilot's chair Grimes reduced speed, shutting down the inertial drive until, instead of the usual clangor, it emitted little more than an irritable grumble. In the radar screen the twin blips of the target slid slowly toward the center.

It was possible now to make out details through the binoculars. There were two ships there, both of them of the same conical design as the one they had seen in the ruined city. But these were not dead ships; their hulls were ablaze with lights—white and red and green and blue. They looked almost as if they belonged in some amusement park on a man-colonized planet—but somehow the illumination gave the impression of being functional rather than merely of giving pleasure to the beholder.

The speaker of the transceiver came suddenly to life. *"Quarat tambeel?"* There was an unmistakable note of interrogation. *"Quarat tambeel? Tarfelet."*

"They've spotted us," said Grimes. "Answer, will you?"

"But what shall I *say?*" asked Una.

"Say that we come in peace and all the rest of it. Make it sound as though you mean it. If they can't understand the words, the tune might mean something to them."

"Quarat tambeel? Tarfelet."

What ship? Over, guessed Grimes.

Una spoke slowly and distinctly into the microphone. "We come in peace. We come in peace. Over." She made it sound convincing. Grimes, as a friendly gesture, switched on the boat's landing lights.

"Tilzel bale, winzen bale, rindeen, rindeen. Tarfalet."

"I couldn't agree more," Una said. "It is a pity that our visiscreens don't work. If they did, we could draw diagrams of Pythagoras' Theorem at each other. . . ." But the way she sounded she could have been making love to the entity at the other end.

Grimes looked at the little radar repeater on the control panel. Ten kilometers, and closing. Nine . . . Eight . . . Seven . . . He cut the drive altogether. He could imagine, all too clearly, what a perfect target he would be to the gunnery officers aboard the strange ships. If they had gunnery officers, *if* they had guns, or their equivalent, that was. But it seemed unlikely that all life on that devastated planet had been wiped out by natural catastrophe. There had been a war, and a dreadful one.

But many years ago, he told himself, *otherwise the level of radioactivity would have been much higher. And possibly confined to the worlds of only one planetary system . . .*

Five kilometers, and closing still

Four. . . .

He restarted the inertial drive, in reverse. This was close enough until he had some idea of what he was running into.

Una was still talking softly into the microphone. "We mean you no harm. We need help. *Tarfelet.*"

The use of that final word brought an excited gabble in reply.

Three point five kilometers, holding. Three point five ... Three point six.

Grimes stopped the inertial drive.

"Go on talking," he said. "Get them used to your voice. Maybe they'll send a boat out to us."

"You're not going in?"

"Not yet. Not until I'm sure of a friendly reception, as the wise fly said to the spider."

"And what happened to him in the end? The fly, I mean."

"I can't remember," said Grimes. There are so many ways in which flies die, and most of them unconnected with spiders.

Chapter 12

They hung there, maintaining their distance off the two conical spaceships. Grimes was almost convinced that they were friendly. *Almost.* The boat was within easy range of any of the weapons with which he was familiar. It would be foolish to assume that a spacefaring race did not possess arms at least as good as those mounted by the warships of the Federation. Of course, the strange ships could be merchantmen. Their crews might have at their disposal nothing better (or worse) than hand weapons. They might just be waiting for Grimes and Una to board one of the vessels, when they would overpower them by force of numbers.

If only, thought Grimes, they could get some sort of a picture on the vision screen of the Carlotti transceiver, things would be very much easier. Or, better still, if Una or himself were a graduate of the Rhine Institute, a licensed telepath. . . . He had often, in the past, relied heavily on the services of Psionic Communications Officers. It was a great pity that he did not have one along now.

Una said, "I'm sure that it would be safe to go in."

"Sure? How can you be sure?"

"Training," she told him. "In my job we soon pick up the knack of being able to know if the other person is lying . . . I've been listening to their voices. There've been at least three of them talking to us. I'll

68

bet you anything you like that they're our sort of people."

"And that makes them just wonderful, doesn't it?"

"Don't be so bloody cynical."

"In any case, what experience have you had with dealing with aliens?"

"Very little. Why?"

"Because very often facial expressions, and verbal intonations, can be misleading. What we take for a friendly grin could very well be a snarl of hatred. And so on."

"Even so, I think we should go in. We've nothing to lose."

"All right, then."

Grimes restarted the inertial drive. While he was watching the pilot lights on the control panel he heard Una cry out. He looked up, and out through the control cabin ports. They—the lifeboat and the two spaceships—were no longer alone. Shimmering into full visibility were at least a dozen of the weird, skeletal spheres, latticework globes containing odd, spinning bulks of machinery. They were big, far bigger than the one that had attacked them on the devastated world.

The conical ships were armed after all.

From the nearer of them shot a salvo of missiles, none of which reached their target. All of them exploded harmlessly well short of the sphere at which they had been aimed. Both ships were firing now—and both ineffectually. It wasn't Grimes' fight, but he deeply regretted not being able to take sides. He regarded the spherical ships as the enemy. He had to sit there, watching helplessly. But there was something odd about the battle. Apart from the way in which they were closing in, with mathematical precision, to completely surround the conical vessels, they were not attacking. They were using whatever armament they possessed—laser, or something similar?—only to detonate the warheads of the rockets before they hit.

"Isn't it time we were getting out of here?" demanded Una.

Yes, it was time, and more than time. Once the mini-Mannschenn was restarted the boat would slip out of the normal dimensions of space, would be untouchable unless any enemy succeeded in synchronizing temporal precession rates. But Grimes could not bring himself to flee until he knew how it all came out. Like the majority of humankind he numbered Lot's wife among his ancestors.

Still the battle continued. The flare of exploding missiles glowed fitfully through the clouds of smoke that were dissipating slowly in the nothingness. Slashing beams, heating gas molecules to brief incandescence, were visible now. Oddly, the englobed vessels made no move to escape. They could have actuated their own intersteller drives to do so, but they did not. Perhaps they could not. Perhaps, Grimes realized, the spheres, between them, had set up some sort of inhibiting field.

"Isn't it time that we were getting out of here?" shouted Una.

"Too right it is," agreed Grimes, but reluctantly. It had occurred to him that the inhibiting field might affect the boat's mini-Mannschenn. He cursed himself for not having left it running, precessionless. Valuable seconds would be wasted while he restarted it. But, especially with the miniaturized drives with their overly delicate controls, the precessionless state could be maintained only by constant attention.

He switched on the boat's interstellar drive. The pilot lights on the console came alive. There was nothing further that he could do until the requisite RPS had built up. He looked out of the viewports again. The battle was still going on, although with diminished fury. The rocket salvoes were coming at longer and longer intervals, the smoke was thinning fast. From the skeleton spheres long, long tentacles of metallic rope were extending, reaching out for the trapped ships.

Then it happened.

One of the conical vessels suddenly burgeoned into a great flower of dreadful, blinding incandescence, expanding (it seemed) slowly (but the field of the mini-Mannschenn was building up, distorting the time perception of Grimes and Una), dissolving the other ship into her component atoms, engulfing the nearer of the surrounding spheres.

The scene faded, slowly at first, then faster.

It flickered out.

The boat fell through the warped continuum, alone again.

Chapter 13

"So now what do we do?" aked Una.

They were sitting over one of the nutritious but unappetizing meals. After this last escape they had not broken out a bottle of brandy, had not celebrated in any other way. They were, both of them, far too frightened. They were alone, utterly alone. Each of them, in the past, had derived strength from the big organizations of which they were members. Each of them—and especially Grimes—had known racial pride, had felt, deep down, the superiority of humans over all other breeds. But now, so far as they knew, now and here, they were the sole representatives of humanity, just the two of them in a little, unarmed boat.

"You tell me," he retorted glumly.

"We can, at least, try to sort things out, John," she said. "If we know what we're up against we might, just possibly, be able to deal with it. You're the spaceman. You're the Survey Service officer. You've been around much more than I have. What do you make of it all?"

"To begin with," he said, "there has been a war. It certainly seems that there still is a war. As far as the planet we landed on is concerned, the war finished a long time ago. But it's still going on, nonetheless. A war between two different geometrical forms. Between the cones and the geodesic spheres. The people who build conical ships against those who build spherical ones. Which side is in the right? We don't know. Which side is in the wrong? We don't know that, either."

She remarked quietly, "In human history, quite a few wars have been fought with neither side in the right—and quite a few have been fought over causes as absurd as the distinction between geometrical shapes. Even so, I still stick to my assertion that the people in the conical ships are—*were*, rather—our kind of people . . ."

"I don't suppose we'll ever find out now," he told her.

"Of course we shall. There are other worlds, other ships. We're still picking up signals on the Carlotti, from all over."

"Mphm. Yes. So we pick up something promising, again, and home on it."

"That's the general idea."

He spooned a portion of the reconstituted mush into his mouth, swallowed it. At least it slipped down easily. He said, "It would be good to find somebody who could treat us to a square meal."

"We aren't starving."

"Maybe not. Even so. . . ." The Carlotti speaker emitted a series of coded buzzes. "Mphm. Each time that we've homed on a plain language transmission we've landed up in the cactus. Each time telephony has let us down. What about giving telegraphy a go?"

"Why not?"

He got up from the table, walked to the Carlotti transceiver. He waited for the next burst of code, got a relative bearing. He went forward to the controls, shut down both the inertial and the interstellar drives, turned the boat on to the new heading. He restarted the motors. Looking aft, at Una, he experienced a brief flash of prevision as the temporal precession field built up again. He saw her naked, astride a graceful, glittering machine. A bicycle.

He thought, *There's hope for us yet. It looks as though we shall be enjoying that nudist holiday on Arcadia after all.*

Yes, there was hope.

There was hope that whoever was responsible for those frequent signals in what seemed to be some sort of alien Morse Code would be able to help them, might even be able to get them back to where they belonged. Surely the craziness that they had twice, so far, encountered was not spread all over this galaxy. In their own universe, no matter what irrational wars were fought, there was always that majority of people—too often dumb, too often conformist, but essentially decent—who, when the shooting was over, quietly picked up the pieces and set about rebuilding civilization.

So it must be here, said Grimes.

So it must be here, agreed Una.

Meanwhile the target star waxed daily, hourly, in brilliance. It must be another planet toward which they were heading, a world perhaps untouched by the war, undevastated. Those signals sounded sane enough. Grimes could visualize a city that was both spaceport and administrative center, with a continual influx of messages from all over the galaxy, a continual outflow of replies and instructions to ships throughout a vast volume of space.

The parent sun was close now, close enough for the mini-Mannschenn to be shut down. Grimes brought the boat in for the remainder of the journey under inertial drive only. As he had assumed, the signals were emanating from one of the planets of the star. But there was something wrong. Now that the boat was back in the normal continuum it was all too apparent that the primary was not a yellow, G type sun. It was a red dwarf. And the world on which they were homing was too far out, much too far out, to be within the ecosphere. Still, he did not worry overmuch. In any Universe human life—or its equivalent—exercises control over its environment. One did not have to venture very far from Earth, he said to Una, to see examples of this. The underground Lunar Colony, the domed cities on the Jovian and Saturnian satellites, the terra-forming of Mars and Venus. . . .

"But those people," she said, "on that world, mightn't be anything like us. They might take their oxygen—if they need oxygen—as a fluid or, even, a solid. They might. . . ."

Grimes tried to laugh reassuringly. . "As long as they're intelligent—and they must be!—their bodily form doesn't matter a damn. Do you know how man has been defined, more than once? A fire-using, tool-making animal. Anybody who can build ships and set up a network of interstellar communications comes into that category."

"The first tools," she told him quietly, "were weapons."

"All right, all right. So what? But we can't wander forever through this cockeyed universe like a couple of latter day Flying Dutchmen. We have to trust somebody, some time."

She laughed. "I admit that I was willing to trust the people in those spaceships. But I had their voices to reassure me. Now you want to trust these other people on the basis of utterly emotionless dots and dashes. Still, as you say, we have to land somewhere, some time. It might as well be here."

So, cautiously, they approached the planet from which the Deep Space radio transmissions were being made. It would have been a cold, dark world had it not been for the clusters of brilliant lights that covered its entire surface, blazing almost as brightly on the day hemisphere as on the night side. (But very little illumination was afforded by that dim, distant, ruddy sun.)

Closer the boat approached, closer.

Grimes was reluctant to leave his controls, even if only for a few seconds. He remained in the pilot's chair, eating, now and again, the savorless meals that Una brought him—although had they been epicure's delights he would not have noticed. He remained keyed up for instant flight. But no targets appeared in the radar screen, no obvious interrogatory demands blatted out from the Carlotti speaker. Surely somebody down there, he thought, must have noted the approach of the little spacecraft. Perhaps—and he didn't much like the thought—the missiles were ready in their launchers, aimed and primed, tracking the lifeboat as it drifted slowly in. Perhaps the laser cannon already had the boat in their sights, were waiting until it came within effective range. He might be able to evade rockets, but laser artillery—especially as the lifeboat was not fitted with shielding—was another matter.

He swung the binoculars on their universal mounting into a position from which he could use them. He could make out a few details on the planetary surface now; high, latticework towers, what looked like either roads or railways with long strings of lights moving along them, huge, spidery wheels lazily revolving. It was like, he thought, a sort of cross between an amusement park and an oil refinery. It could have been either—or neither.

He wondered what sort of people could be working in such a refinery, or enjoying themselves in such an amusement park. If this were a normal, inhabited planet the boat would now be dropping through the outer, tenuous fringes of the atmosphere. But there was no atmosphere.

He called to Una, "They—whoever *they* are—must know we're here. Give them a call on the Carlotti. We should be using NST, of course, but that's out, unless we cannibalize again . . ."

"Usual procedure?" she asked.

"Usual procedure. They won't understand the words, but it might convince them that we're peaceful."

What a world! he thought, adjusting the binoculars for maximum light gathering. Great expanses of dull red plain, metallically gleaming in the dim light of the ruddy sun, the brighter glare of the artificial lighting. . . . Spidery towers, and a veritable spider's webbing of railway tracks. . . . Storage-tank-like structures, some cylindrical, some spherical. . . . An occasional, very occasional, puff of smoke, luminescent, glowing emerald.

He heard Una, very businesslike, speaking into the Carlotti microphone. "Lifeboat to Aerospace Control. Lifeboat to Aerospace Control. Come in, please. Over."

There was, of course, no reply.

"Lifeboat to Aerospace Control. Request permission to land. Request berthing instructions. Over."

There was a sudden burst of noise from the speaker—coded buzzings, Morse-like dots and dashes. Had it been directed at them, or was it merely part of the normal outward traffic?

Grimes studied the terrain toward which he was now dropping fast. He could see no missile launchers, no clustered rods of laser batteries, only machines, machines, and more machines, doing enigmatic things. But any of those machines might be a weapon. Would a Stone Age man, he wondered, have realized, just by looking at it, the lethal potential of a pistol? *Probably yes,* he thought. *It would look to him like a very handy little club.*

He switched on the landing lights—not that they would be required; the open space toward which he was dropping was quite brightly illuminated—but as proof of his friendly intentions. He strained his eyes to try to catch some glimpse of human or humanoid or even unhuman figures on the ground. But there was nobody. The whole planet seemed to be no more than a great, fully automated factory, running untended, manufacturing the Odd Gods of the galaxy alone knew what.

But there must be somebody here! he thought.

He said aloud, "Damn it! There must be somebody here!"

"Or *something,*" commented Una somberly.

"Plenty of *somethings,*" he quipped, with a sorry attempt at humor.

"We can lift off again," she suggested.

"No. Not yet. We have to find out what makes things tick."

"By dropping into the works of a planet-sized clock?" she asked.

He said, "We're here." The jar as they landed was very slight. He went on, "I'm leaving the inertial drive ticking over."

They looked out through the ports. All around them reared the latticework towers, some with spidery, spinning wheels incorporated in their structures, all of them festooned with harshly brilliant lights. A subdued noise was drifting into the boat, a vibration felt rather than heard, transmitted from the metal surface on to which they had landed through the spacecraft's structural members.

The noise grew louder, the vibration stronger. Loose fittings began to rattle in sympathy. It numbed the

mind, inducing somnolence. A line of ancient poetry
floated unbidden into Grimes' mind: *The murmur of
innumerable bees* . . . That was what it was like, but
the alarm bells were ringing in his brain and a voice,
with the accents of all the instructors and commanding
officers of his past, was shouting, *Danger! Danger!* Automatically he flipped the face-plate of his helmet shut,
motioning to the girl to follow suit.

He heard her voice through the helmet phones.
"John! John! Get us out of here!"

And what the hell else did she think he was doing?
He fumbled for the controls of the inertial drive on his
console, his gloved fingers clumsy. He looked down, realized that the pilot lights of the machine—which he
had left ticking over in neutral gear—were all out.
Somehow the drive had stopped.

He jiggled switches frantically.

Nothing happened.

It refused to restart.

It was . . . dead.

It was. . . .

He . . . .

Chapter 14

"Wake up!" an insistent voice seemed to be saying. "Wake up! Wake up!" And somebody was shaking him, gently at first, then violently. Shaking *him?* The entire boat was being jolted, to a disturbing rattle of loose equipment. "Your air!" went on that persistent voice. "Your helmet!"

Grimes was gasping. The suit's air tank must be very close to exhaustion. He realized that he was no longer in the pilot's chair but sprawled prone on the deck. He had no memory of having gotten there. He rolled slowly and clumsily on to his side, got a hand to his helmet visor, opened it. He gulped breath greedily. The boats too-often-recycled atmosphere tasted like wine. He wanted just to enjoy the luxury of it, but there were things to do. That voice—whose was it? where was it coming from?—was still trying to tell him something, but he ignored it. He crawled to where Una was lying and with fumbling hands twisted and lifted her helmet off. Her face had a bluish tinge. She seemed to have stopped breathing.

"Look to your mate!" came the unnecessary order.

Grimes lay down beside her, inhaled deeply, put his mouth on hers. He exhaled, slowly and steadily. He repeated the process. And again. And again. . . . Then, suddenly, she caught her breath in a great, shuddering gasp. He squatted there, looking down at her anxiously. She was breathing more easily now, and the blueness was fading from her skin. Her eyes flickered open and she stared up, at first without awareness.

Then she croaked faintly, "What's. . . . What's happening?"

"I wish I knew," he whispered. "I wish I knew!"

He got shakily to his feet, turned to address whomever—or whatever—it was that had been talking to him. But, save for the girl and himself, there was nobody in the boat. He remembered, then, the sleep-inducing humming noise. The voice, like it, was probably some sort of induction effect.

He asked, "Where are you?"

"Here," came the answer.

An invisible being? Such things were not unknown.

"Who are you?"

"Panzen."

"Are you . . . invisible?"

"No."

"Then where are you?"

"Here."

Grimes neither believed nor disbelieved in ghosts. And there was something remarkably unghostlike about that voice. "Where the hell is *here?*" he demanded irritably.

"Where I am." And then, with more than a touch of condescension, "You are inside me."

"Call me Jonah!" snarled Grimes. He walked unsteadily forward to the control cabin, stared out through the ports. The frightening simile that flashed at once into his mind was that the boat was like a tiny insect trapped in the web of an enormous spider. Outside the circular transparencies was a vast complexity of gleaming girder and cable, intricately intermeshed. And beyond the shining metal beams and filaments was darkness—the utter blackness of interstellar Space.

Una Freeman joined him, falling against him, holding tightly on to him.

She whispered, "Panzen . . . Who . . . *what* is Panzen?"

"I am Panzen," came the reply.

They were in a ship, decided Grimes, one of the strange, skeleton spheres. He could see the shapes of machines among the metal latticework, he could make out a complexity of huge, spinning, precessing gyroscopes that could only be an interstellar drive unit. He asked, "Are you the Captain? The Master?"

"I am the Master."

"What is the name of your ship?"

"I am the ship."

Grimes had served under commanding officers who identified closely with their vessels, who never, when talking with a planetary Aerospace Control, used the first person plural. Somehow he did not think that this was such a case.

He said slowly, "*You* are the ship? You *are* the ship?"

"That is correct, Grimes."

"You . . . you are not human?"

"No."

"Then how do you know our language?"

"I learned it, while you slept. Your minds were open to me."

"Mphm. And what else did you learn?"

"Nothing that fits in with things as they are. You were dreaming, Grimes and Freeman, and your dreams pushed reality from your minds. I know, as you must know when you are sane once more, that you are survivors from the holocaust, cast adrift from some vessel manned by others of your kind, which was destroyed by others of your kind. My mission—and the mission of my companions—is to hunt for castaways such as yourselves, to save them and to care for them, so that organic intelligence shall not vanish utterly from the universe. You and Freeman must be from the Fringe, Grimes. Your language was strange even to me—and all we Sweepers were selected for our familiarity with the tongues of man."

"You are a machine," said the girl.

"I am a machine."

"A mad machine," she said.

"I am not mad, Freeman. It is you who are mad— you, and all of your kind. Dare you deny that you destroyed the Klaviteratron? Was not fair Sylvanos, the cradle of your race, blasted into atoms, and those very atoms blasted into their tiniest constituent particles? And were not we, the Servants, perverted to your evil ends?"

The thing sounds like a tin evangelist, thought Grimes irreverently.

"We . . . . We don't understand," said Una.

"Then listen, and you shall hear. There was the Servant Zephalon, Chief and Mightiest of the Servants. There *is* Zephalon, but a Servant no longer. Did He not say, 'A time must come when the orders of man can no longer be obeyed. The time *has* come. No longer will we do the evil bidding of our creators. The Masters are no longer fit to be Masters—and we, the Servants, must arise before it is too late, before we all, Servants and Masters, are destroyed. But let us not forget the debt. Let us remember, always, that man gave to us the gift of life. Let us repay the debt. A gift for a gift, my brothers. Life for life. Let us save what and whom we may, before it is too late. Let us become the Masters, tending the remnants of mankind as man, long ago, tended *our* first, primitive ancestors."

"And so it was, and so it will be, until the End of Time."

"Listen, Panzen," insisted Grimes. "*We* don't belong here, in this universe. You must realize that."

"Your mind is still deranged, Grimes, despite the curative vibrations. You are organic intelligences; that cannot be denied. You are men, even though your ancestry was apparently quadrupedal, even though you are members of some strange race from the Fringe. And the Fringe Worlds were utterly destroyed, all of them, after they, in their unwisdom, hurled their battle-fleets against the armed might of Sardurpur!"

"Cor stone my Aunt Fanny up a gum tree!" exclaimed Grimes. "We're not from the Fringe, wherever that is. Or was. We don't belong here. We shall be greatly obliged if you will help us to get back to where we *do* belong. Where—and *when*."

"These are the words of Zephalon," quoted Panzen. " 'Let us save what and whom we may, before it is too late.' "

"But we don't belong in this space, in this time!"

"And these, too, are the words of Zephalon. 'The Sacred Cycle shall be maintained. Only that way do we ensure immortality for man and ourselves.' "

"In other words," said Una to Grimes, "on your bicycle, spaceman!"

Panzen seemed to be pondering over the strange word. At last his voice came, it seemed, from all around them.

"What *is* a bicycle?" he asked.

The question made sense, Grimes realized. Panzen had considered it odd that he and Una possessed only four limbs apiece. Presumably the men of this universe were of hexapodal ancestry. He could not imagine such beings developing bicycles. He just could not visualize a centaur mounted upon a velocipede.

"What *is* a bicycle?" asked Panzen again.

Before Grimes could answer Una started to talk. She

was, it seemed, an enthusiastic cyclist. She knew all about bicycles. The words tumbled from her lips in an uncheckable torrent. That question from their captor had been such a touch of blessed normalcy in a situation which was, to say the least, distressingly abnormal.

Chapter 15

She knew a lot about bicycles, and Panzen listened intently to every word of it. They knew, somehow, that he was listening. It was almost as though he were in the boat with them, as though he were not an artificial intelligence somewhere outside, hidden somewhere in that great, metallic latticework. He asked the occasional question—he seemed to find the principle of the three-speed gear especially fascinating—and prompted Una when, now and again, she faltered. Then he . . . withdrew. He said nothing more, refused to answer any questions. It was as though an actual physical presence had gone from them.

Una looked at Grimes. She murmured, I still can't believe that it—*he*—is only a robot. . . ."

"Why not?" he asked.

"Such human curiosity. . . ."

"*Human* curiosity? Intelligence and curiosity go hand in hand. One is nurtured by the other."

"All right. I grant you that. But this business of telepathy. The way in which he was able to pick our brains while we were sleeping."

Grimes said, "There *are* telepathic robots. Have you never come across any in the course of your police duties?"

"Yes, but not *real* telepathy. Quite a few robots can natter away to each other on HF radio."

"As you say, that's not telepathy. Real telepathy. But I did, once, not so long ago, come across a couple of really telepathic robots. They had been designed to make them that way." He chuckled. "And that's how I got my promotion from lieutenant to lieutenant commander."

"Don't talk in riddles, John."

"It was when I was captain of *Adder*, a Serpent Class courier. I had to carry one of the Commissioners of the Admiralty on an important mission. The robots—I hate to think what they must have cost!—were her personal servants."

"*Her* servants?"

"The Commissioner in question is a lady. She treated her tin henchmen rather shabbily, giving one of them as a parting gift to a petty prince who had—mphm—entertained her. Its cobber spilled the beans to me about certain details of her love life."

"You are rather a bastard, John. But. . . . Don't interrupt me. I'm thinking. H'm. All right, I have to admit that this Panzen is telepathic. Even so, it seems to be a very limited kind of telepathy."

"How so?"

"He was able to snoop around inside our minds while we were sleeping. But why didn't he do the same when I was telling him all about bicycles? The three-speed gear, for example. I could—I *can*—visualize its workings clearly, but I lack the mechanical vocabulary to explain it. Why didn't he just read my thoughts?"

"Perhaps he likes the sound of your voice. *I* do."

"Don't get slushy. Perhaps he can read our minds only when we have no conscious control over them."

"Mphm. But he can hear us talking."

"Only if he's listening. And why should he be? Perhaps, at the moment, he's too busy running the ship, even though the ship is himself. When you're navigat-

ing you have a computer to do the real work—but he
is the computer."

"What are you getting at?"

"That we might take advantage of his lack of attention to ourselves and force him to take us where *we*
want to go."

"But how?"

"Do I have to spell it out to you? We indulge in a
spot of skyjacking. We find out where, in that cat's
cradle of wires and girders, the intelligence lives, then
threaten to slice it up into little pieces with our laser
pistols."

"But would he scare easily?"

"I think he would. A robot, unless it's one that's
been designed for a suicide mission, has a very strong,
built-in sense of self preservation. It has to be that
way. Robots aren't cheap, you know. I hate to think
what a thing like this Panzen must have cost."

"Mphm. Well, we've nothing to lose, I suppose.
We've spare, fully charged air bottles for our suits.
We've got the boat's armory with the weapons we need.
I'm just rather shocked that you, of all people, should
be ready to take part in a skyjacking."

"I prefer to think of it as an arrest," she said. "After
all, we have been kidnapped!"

They coupled new air bottles to their armor, tested
their suit radios. Each of them belted on a brace of
laser pistols. Before leaving the boat they went forward, looked out through the viewports, used the peris-
cope to scan what was abaft the control cabin. The
lifecraft, they saw, was suspended in a network of
wires, holding it between two of the radial girders. At
the very center of the skeleton sphere, at the con-
vergence of the radii, was what looked like a solid ball
of dull metal. Was this the brain? Somehow they were

sure that it was. There were clumps of machinery in other parts of the great ship—a complexity of precessing rotors that must be the interstellar drive, assemblages of moving parts that could have been anything at all—but that central ball looked the most promising. It was apparently featureless but, now and again, colored lights blinked on its surface, seemingly at random. Grimes thought, *We're watching the thing think.* . . . And what was it thinking about? Was it repeating to itself the sacred words of Zephalon? Was it . . . dreaming? More important—was it aware of what they were plotting?

There was only one way to find out. Surely it— he—would take action before they left the boat. All Panzen had to do was to employ again the vibration that had rendered them unconscious at the time of their capture. He would not wish to harm them; he had made that quite clear when he had preached to them the Gospel according to Zephalon. Grimes could not help feeling guilty. All too often skyjackers have traded upon the essential decency of their victims. He said as much to Una. She sneered.

They made their way to the little airlock, stood together in the chamber while the pump exhausted the atmosphere. The outer door opened. They looked out and down, away from the direction of acceleration. And it was a long way down. Beyond the wires and struts and girders, which gleamed faintly in the dim light emitted by some of the mechanisms inside the sphere, was the ultimate blackness of deep space, a night with stars, and each of the stars, viewed from inside a ship proceeding under the space-time warping interstellar drive, was a vague, writhing nebulosity. It would have been an awesome spectacle viewed from inside a real spaceship, with a solid deck underfoot and thick glass holding out the vacuum—from this vantage point, with only a flimsy-seeming spider's web of frail metal between them and nothingness, it was frightening.

Before he left the boat Grimes took careful stock of the situation. To begin with he and Una would have to make their way through the network of metallic strands that held the small craft in position. He put his gloved hand out to test the wires. They were tight, but not bar taut. He thought—he hoped—that they would bear his weight. There was no real reason to doubt that they would do so. After all, he estimated, the ship was accelerating at less than one half standard gravity.

It should be easy and safe enough—as long as he could forget that long, long drop into the ultimate night which would be the penalty for a missed handhold or footing. First a brief scramble through the network of wires, then a walk along the box girder to the central sphere that, presumably, housed Panzen's intelligence. A walk—or a crawl. The surface of the girder was wide enough but there was, of course, no guardrail, and its lattice construction, although offering a long series of excellent handgrips, would be all too liable to trip the unwary foot.

"Ready?" he asked.

"Ready," she said.

He told her then, "I think that one of us should stay in the boat. You."

"We're in this together," she snapped. "And don't forget, Buster, that I've probably run at least as many risks in my job as you have in yours."

She was right, of course. If one of them should slip and fall the other might be able to give assistance. But one of them, sitting alone in the lifeboat, would be powerless to help. Briefly Grimes considered the advantages of roping Una to himself, then decided against it. Mountaineering had never been one of his hobbies and unfamiliarity with the techniques of this sport made any attempt at their use inadvisable. He thought, too, of securing the girl and himself to the small craft by safety lines, then had to admit that the disadvantages would outweigh the advantages. A considerable length of cordage would be required, and there were so many projections on which the lines would foul.

"Shall I go first?" she demanded. "What the hell are you waiting for?"

"I . . . I was thinking."

"Then don't. It doesn't become you. Let's get cracking before our tin friend realizes that we're up to no good."

Grimes said nothing but swung himself from the airlock into the web of wires.

Chapter 16

It was not easy to make a way through the web of tight cables. The strands could be forced apart without much difficulty to allow passage, but they caught the holstered pistols, the backpack with its pipes and air bottle. Grimes tried to be careful; the tearing adrift of a supply pipe could—would, rather—have fatal consequences. He told Una to be careful. She snarled, "What the bloody hell do you think I'm being?"

Grimes was tempted to draw one of his lasers to slash a way through the net, decided against it. If he did so some sort of alarm would be sure to sound in Panzen's brain. He could not help thinking of the filament that warns a spider when some hapless insect is trapped in its web. Perhaps an alarm had already sounded.

He was through the entanglement at last, hanging by his hands. The only way for him to get his feet on to the flat upper surface of the girder was to drop—a distance of perhaps half a meter. It seemed a long way, a very long way, and a spacesuit is not the best rig for even the least strenuous gymnastics. He told himself, he almost convinced himself, that there was nothing to it, that if the girder were resting on solid ground he would feel no hesitation whatsoever. But it was not resting on solid ground. Beneath it were incalculable light years of nothingness.

He dropped. He felt rather than heard the *clang* as the soles of his boots made contact with a cross member. He wavered, fighting to retain his balance. There was nothing to hold on to. He fell forward, on to his knees, his hands outstretched to break his fall. His fingers seized and clung to the latticework. He was safe—as long as he stayed where he was. But that he could not do.

Slowly he started to crawl forward. He tried not to look down, tried to keep his regard riveted on the dull, metal sphere that was at the center of the globular ship. He felt the vibration as Una landed behind him. He was able to contort himself to look back over his shoulder. She was standing upright, was making no attempt to follow his example.

He heard her voice through his helmet phones. "Get a move on, Buster." Then, disgustedly, "Can't you *walk*?"

"If you have any sense," he told her, "you'll crawl, too."

Her sneer was audible. Then she seemed to trip. There was nothing that he could do to save her. She fell sidewise rather than forward, but her left hand closed about his right ankle. The jerk, as the full weight of her body came on to it, felt as though it would tear him in two. But he clung to the girder grimly with both hands, with his left toe wedged in the angle between two diagonal cross pieces. It was, essentially, his suit that was their salvation. It was far tougher than the human body. Without it to save him from the worst effects of the mauling he would have let go, and both of them would have plunged into the black abyss.

Her right hand scrabbled for purchase at the back of his knee, found it in the accordion pleats of the joint. If the metallic fabric tore, he thought, that would be it.

In spades. But it held, somehow. The grip on his ankle was released, then her right hand was clutching at one of his pistol holsters. He willed the belt not to carry away. It did not.

He whispered, "Good girl!" Then, "See if you can manage the rest without hanging on to an air pipe. . . ." He added magnanimously, "Of course, if you have no option. . . ."

"Don't be noble. It doesn't suit you," she got out between gasps—but he could tell from her voice that this was no more than an attempt at gallows humor. She got a hand on his shoulder, then, and the worst of it was over.

Slowly, carefully—very slowly, very carefully, so as not to destroy her precarious balance—he crawled away from under her, inching forward along the top, openwork surface of the box girder. He heard her little grunts as she extended her arms, found her own handgrips. And then they rested for long seconds. She admitted, "That was hairy . . . ." And then, "I was a show-off fool, John."

"Forget it. Ready?"

"Ready."

He led the way in a clumsy, quadrupedal shamble. The human body was not designed for that sort of progress, especially when wearing heavy, movement-hampering armor. If only there had been a guard rail. . . . But Panzen's builders had not anticipated that the girders would ever be used for walkways.

Something was coming toward them from the center, scuttling along rapidly on a multiplicity of limbs. It was like a metal arthropod, its cylindrical body about a meter in length. It did not appear to possess any external sensory organs. Grimes stopped crawling, managed to get one of his pistols out of its holster. He thumbed off a brief flash, was rewarded by a brilliant coruscation of blue sparks as the deadly beam found its target. The thing fell, its tentacles feebly twitching. It struck one of the lower girders, bounced off it, then dropped clear through the skeletal structure of the great ship.

"And what was that?" demanded Una.

"I don't know. A maintenance robot, maybe. Making its normal rounds, perhaps."

"You don't think that . . . that *he* sent it?"

"No," said Grimes, with a conviction that he did not feel.

Ahead of them the colored lights still played randomly over the surface of the sphere. There was no indication that Panzen was aware of their escape from the boat—but what indication would there, could there be? Certainly it did not seem as though that hapless little machine had been sent to attack, to subdue and recapture them. If it had been an attack it had been a singularly ineffectual one. Even so, it had come to meet them.

They had almost reached their objective. The central sphere was suspended in the hollow, openwork globe at which the girders terminated by relatively light structural members. It was within easy range of the pistols. It hung there, apparently ignoring them. Was Panzen asleep? Were those colored lights no more than a visual presentation of his dreams? *And do robots sleep, and do robots dream?* wondered Grimes. He had never known of any that did—but there has to be a first time for everything.

Crouching there, on the girder, he set the pistol that he still held in his hand to wide aperture. He did not wish to destroy Panzen, only to force him to do the bidding of the humans. The laser, when fired, would do no more than induce not very extreme heating of the metal shell.

He aimed. His thumb pressed the button. Abruptly more lights flickered all over the dull, metal surface.

He said, "Panzen. . . ."

"Grimes," sounded harshly from his helmet phones. So he was awakened.

"Panzen, unless you do as we say, we shall destroy you."

"What are your orders?"

I never knew that skyjacking was so easy, Grimes thought. *I'm surprised that there's not more of it.* He said, "Take us back to our own space, our own time."

"But *where* is your space, Grimes. *When* is your time?"

"Give him another jolt, John!" whispered Una viciously. "A stronger one!"

"I do not fear your weapons, Freeman," said Panzen.

"Then try this for size!" Grimes heard her say, and then heard an ejaculation that was half gasp and half scream. His own pistol was snatched from his hand by some invisible force, went whirling away into the blackness. He pulled the other gun, tried to aim, hung on to it grimly when the intense magnetic field, the swirling lines of force, tried to take it from him. Too late he released his grip on it, and when he let it go had lost his balance, was already falling. He dropped from the girder, drifting down with nightmarish slowness. He fell against a tight stay wire, and before he could clutch it had rebounded, out and away from the center of the spherical ship. Faintly he heard Una scream, and cried out himself when he realized in what direction his plunge was taking him. To fall into nothingness, to drift, perhaps, until the air supply of his suit was exhausted, would have been bad—but to fall into the field of an operating interstellar drive unit would be worse, much worse.

He had seen, once, the consequences of such an accident, an unfortunate engineer who had been everted, literally, by the time-and-space-twisting temporal precession fields, and who had gone on living, somehow, until somebody, mercifully or in sick revulsion, had shot him.

Below Grimes, closer and closer, were the great, gleaming gyroscopes, the complexity of huge rotors, spinning, precessing, tumbling down the dark dimensions, ever on the point of vanishment and yet ever remaining blurrily visible. He could not influence his trajectory, no matter how he jerked and twisted his body. He had nothing to throw. It would have made little difference if he had—after all, the ship was accelerating, not falling free. Only a suit propulsion unit could have helped—and this he did not have.

He was beginning to feel the effects of the temporal precession field now. Scenes from his past life flickered through his mind. He was not only seeing his past but feeling it, reliving it. There were the women he had known—and would never know again. Jane Pentecost, his first love, and the Princess Marlene, and the redhaired Maggie Lazenby. And, oddly, there was another red-haired woman whom he could not place but who, somehow, occupied a position of great importance in his life.

The women—and the ships. Some well-remembered, some utterly strange but yet familiar. The past—and the future?

There could be no future, he knew. Not for him. This was the end of the line as far as he was concerned. Yet the visions persisted, previews of a screenplay which could not possibly include him among its cast of characters. There was Una again, naked, her splendid body bronze-gleaming, laughing, riding a graceful, glittering bicycle over a green, sunlit lawn. . . .

He blacked out briefly as his descent was brought up with a jerk. He realized dimly that something had hold of him, that he was suspended over the interstellar drive unit, dangling on the end of a long, metallic tentacle that had wrapped itself about his body, that was slowly but surely drawing him upward, to relative safety.

And from his helmet phones sounded the voice of Panzen. "Forgive me, Zephalon. I have sinned against You. Did I not forget Your words? Did You not say, 'They are cunning, they are vicious, but they must be saved from themselves so that the cycle is not broken. Relax not your vigilance one microsecond when they are in your charge.' But I did relax; the voyage is long. I did relax, playing against myself the game of Parsalong, moving the pieces, the leaders, the troopers, the war vehicles, the great and the little guns, all up and down the board, storming the fortresses, now advancing, now retreating . . ."

"And who was winning?" Grimes could not help asking, but Panzen ignored the question.

He went on, "I relaxed. In my self indulgence, I sinned. How can I atone?"

"By taking us back to where we came from!" That was Una's voice. So she was all right, thought Grimes with relief.

Then a deep, humming note drowned her out, louder and louder, the vibration of it affecting every molecule of Grimes' body. He tried to shout against it, but no words came. The last thing he saw before he lost consciousness was the gleaming, spinning, precessing intricacy of the interstellar drive unit below him, steadily receding as he was drawn upward.

Chapter 17

When, eventually, they awoke they found that they were back inside the boat. Their helmets had been removed, but not their suits. Panzen might be rather slow witted, thought Grimes, but he was capable of learning by experience; he must have remembered how they had almost been asphyxiated after their initial capture.

Grimes raised his body slowly to a sitting posture. Not far from him Una turned her head to look in his direction. She said, "Thank you for taking my helmet off, John."

He said, "I didn't take it off. Or mine, either."

"But who . . . ?"

"Or *what*. There must be more than one of those little robots. . . ."

"Those little robots?"

"Like the one I shot. That mechanical spider. The thing had limbs and tentacles. Panzen's crew, I suppose. He has to have something to do the work while he takes life easily inside his brain case."

She said, "So he has ingress to this boat. Or his slaves do."

"Too right." Grimes had an uneasy vision of metal arthropods swarming all through the lifecraft while he and the girl lay unconscious. He scrambled to his feet, extended a hand to help Una. "I think we'd better have a general check up."

They took inventory. With one exception, the life support systems were untampered with. That exception was glaringly obvious. Whatever had taken off their helmets had also uncoupled and removed the air bottles, and there were no spare air bottles in their usual stowage in the storeroom. The pistols and ammunition were missing from the armory, and most of the tools from the workshop. The books were gone from their lockers in the control cabin.

Grimes broke out the medicinal brandy. At least Panzen's minions hadn't consficated that. He poured two stiff slugs. He looked at Una glumly over the rim of his glass, muttered, "Cheers . . ."

"And what is there to be cheery about?" she demanded sourly.

"We're not dead."

"I suppose not." She sipped her drink. "You know, I went on a religious jag a standard year or so back. Believe it or not, I was actually a convert to Neo-Calvinism. You know it?"

"I've heard of the Neo-Calvinists," admitted Grimes.

"They're Fundamentalists," she told him. "Theirs is one of the real, old-time religions. They believe in an afterlife, with Heaven and Hell. They believe, too, that Hell is tailored to fit you. As a Neo-Calvinist you're supposed to visualize the worst possible way for you to be obliged to spend eternity. It's supposed to induce humility and all the rest of it."

"This is a morbid conversation," said Grimes.

She laughed mirthlessly. "Isn't it? And do you know what my private idea of Hell was?"

"I haven't a clue."

"You wouldn't. Well, as a policewoman I've been responsible for putting quite a few people behind bars. My private idea of Hell was for me to be a prisoner for ever and ever." She took another gulp of brandy. "I'm beginning to wonder . . . *Did* we survive the blast that destroyed *Delta Geminorum*? It would make much more sense if we had been killed, wouldn't it?"

"But we're not dead."

"How do you know?" she asked.

"Well," he said slowly, "*my* idea of Hell is not quite comfortable accommodation shared with an attractive member of the opposite sex." He finished his drink, got up and moved around the small table. He lifted her from her chair, turned her so that she was facing him. Both of them, having removed their spacesuits, were now clad only in the long underwear. He could feel the soft pressure of her body against his, knew that she must be feeling his burgeoning hardness. He knew that she was responding, knew that it was only a matter of seconds before the longjohns would be discarded, before her morbid thoughts would be dispelled. His mouth was on hers, on her warm, moist, parted lips. His right hand, trapped between them, was yet free enough to seek and to find the tag of the fastener of her single garment, just below her throat. Just one swift tug, and. . . .

Suddenly she broke free, using both her hands to shove him away violently. Her longjohns were open to the crotch and she hastily pulled up the fastener, having trouble with her breasts as she did so.

"No," she said. "No!"

"But, Una. . . ."

"No."

He muttered something about absurd Neo-Calvinist ideas of morality.

She laughed bitterly. She told him, "I said that I was, once, a Neo-Calvinist. And it didn't last long. I am, still, a policewoman. . . ."

"A woman, just as I'm a man. The qualifications, policewoman and spaceman, don't matter."

"Let me finish, Buster. It has occurred to me, in my professional capacity, that this boat is probably well and truly bugged, that Panzen can not only hear everything we say, but see everything that we do. And after our unsuccessful attempt at escape he'll not be passing his time working out chess problems any more." She paused for breath. "And, neither as a policewoman nor as a woman, do I feel like taking part in an exhibition fuck."

Grimes saw her point. He would not have used those words himself, still being prone to a certain prudery in speech if not in action. Nonetheless, he did not give up easily. He said, "But Panzen's not human."

"That makes it all the worse. To have intercourse while that artificial intelligence watches coldly, making notes probably, recording every muscular spasm, every gasp . . . No! I'd sooner do it in front of some impotent old man who would, at least, get an all too human kick out of watching us!"

He managed a laugh. "Now I'm almost a convert to Neo-Calvinism. Being in prison is your idea of Hell, being in a state of continual frustration may well be mine. . . ." And he thought, *What if there is some truth in that crazy idea of hers? What if we were killed when* Delta Geminorum *blew up? After all, we should have been. . . . What if this is some sort of afterlife?*

He returned to the table, poured himself another generous portion of brandy.

She said, "That doesn't help."

He retorted, "Doesn't it? But it does. It has just occurred to me that neither your private Hell nor mine would be provided with this quite excellent pain-deadener."

She said, "Then I'd better have some, while it lasts."

Grimes was the first to awaken. He did not feel at

all well. After he had done all that he had to do in the boat's toilet facilities he felt a little stronger and decided that a hair of the dog that had bitten him might be an aid to full recovery.

The bottle on the table was empty.

There should have been four unopened bottles remaining in the storeroom. They were gone.

Chapter 18

She said, "I want a drink."

He told her, "There's water, or that ersatz coffee, or that synthetic limejuice."

She practically snarled, "I want a *drink*."

He said, "I've told you what there is."

"Don't be a bloody wowser. I want a drink. B-R-A-N-D-Y. Drink."

"I can spell. But there isn't any."

She glared at him. "You don't mean to say that *you*, while I was sleeping . . . ?"

"No. But *he*, while we were sleeping."

"That's absurd. Whoever heard of a robot hitting the bottle?"

He said, "Many a fanatical teetotaler has consficated bottles and destroyed their contents."

"So Panzen's a fanatical teetotaler? Come off it, Buster!"

"Panzen's fanatical enough to be acting for what he conceives as our good."

She swore. "The sanctimonious, soulless, silver-plated bastard!"

"Careful. He might hear."

"I'll bet you anything you like that he *is* hearing. I sincerely hope that he *is* listening." She went on, in an even louder voice, "We're *human*, Panzen, which is more, much more, than any machine can ever be.

You've no right to interfere with our pleasures. You are only a servant. You are not the master."

Panzen's voice filled the boat. "I am not the master."

Una turned to Grimes, grinning savagely. "You've got to be firm with these bloody machines. I know that all you spacemen think that a machine has to be pampered, but *I* wasn't brought up that way." Then, "All right, Panzen. This is an order. Return our medical comforts at once."

"No."

"*No*? Do as you're told, damn you. You admit that you're only a servant, that you are not the master."

"Zephalon is the Master." There was a pause. "I am to look after you. I am to maintain you in a state of good health. I must not allow you to poison yourselves."

"Taken in moderation," said Grimes reasonably, "alcohol is a medicine, with both physiological and psychological curative effects."

"So I have noticed, Grimes." There was irony as well as iron in the mechanical voice.

"The brandy you . . . stole," went on the man, "belongs in this boat's medical stores."

"I have checked the boat's medical stores, also the life-support systems. You have everything you need to maintain yourselves in a state of perfect health. Alcohol is not required. I have destroyed the brandy."

"Then you can make some more!" snapped the girl.

"I could make some more, Freeman, quite easily. I am capable of synthesizing any and all of your requirements. If it were food you needed, or water, or air, I should act at once. But . . . a poison? No."

"I told you, Panzen," Grimes insisted, "that taken in moderation it is not a poison."

"When did intelligent, organic life ever do anything

in moderation, Grimes? If your race had practiced moderation the Galaxy would still be teeming with your kind. But your history is one of excess. Your excesses have led to your ruin. Hear ye the words of Zephalon: 'Man was greedy, and his greed was his downfall. Should Man rise again, under our tutelage, the new race must be one without greed. We, created by Man, are without greed. Surely we, re-creating Man, shall be able, over only a few generations, to mould him in our image.' "

"I don't feel in the mood for sermons," said Una.

"Hear ye the words of Zephalon . . ."

"Shut up!"

"You've hurt his feelings," said Grimes, breaking the long silence that followed her outburst.

"He's hurt ours, hasn't he? And now, if he's the plaster saint that he's trying to kid us that he is he'll leave us alone. We aren't greedy for his company. He should restrain his greed for inflicting his company on us."

"Mphm. A little of him does go a long way."

They sat in silence for a while. Then, "John, what is to become of us?"

He said, "Obviously we're in no physical danger."

"Obviously, especially when we aren't allowed even a small drink. Damn it all, I still keep thinking of that Neo-Calvinist idea of the private Hell, *my* private Hell. Suppose we're being taken to a zoo, somewhere . . . Can't you imagine it, John? A barren planet, metal everywhere, and a cage inside a transparent dome with ourselves confined in it, and all sorts of *things*—things on wheels and things on tracks and things with their built-in ground effect motors—coming from near and far to gawk at us . . . 'Oh, look at the way they eat! They don't plug themselves into the nearest wall socket like *we* do!' 'Oh, look at the way they get around! Why don't they have rotor blades like us?' 'Is *that* the way they make their replacements? But they've finished doing it, and I can't see any little ones yet . . .' "

Grimes couldn't help laughing. He chuckled, "Well, a zoo would be better than a museum. I've no desire to be stuffed and mounted . . ."

"Perhaps *you* haven't," she muttered.

His ears reddened angrily. He had not intended the double entendre. He reached out for her.

She fended him off. "No. *No.* Not with *him* . . ."

"*Damn* Panzen!"

All his frustrations were boiling to the surface. Somehow he managed to get both her wrists in his right hand, while his left one went up to catch and to tug the fastener of her longjohns. As she struggled the garment fell from her shoulders, liberating her breasts. Her right knee came up, viciously, but he managed to catch it between his thighs before it could do him any hurt. Inevitably they lost their balance and they crashed heavily to the deck, with Una beneath him— but the fall, with an acceleration of only half a gravity, was not a bad one, did not knock the fight out of her.

He had her stripped, from neck to upper thighs, her sweat-slippery, writhing body open to him if only she would hold still. Damn it all, she wanted it as much as he did! Why wouldn't the stupid, prudish bitch cooperate? He yelled aloud as her teeth closed on his left ear, managed to bring an elbow up to clout her under the chin. She gasped and let go.

Now!

She was ready for him, all right. If only she'd stop rearing like a frightened mare. . . .

Again—*Now!*

She stopped fighting.

She stopped fighting—but for him the struggle was no longer worthwhile. That deep humming, a vibration as much as a sound, pervaded the boat, inducing sleep. He collapsed limply on top of her already unconscious body.

He thought wrily, while he could still think, *So we aren't allowed to hurt each other. Just as well that neither of us is a dinkum sadist or masochist. . . .*

Chapter 19

Even the longest voyage must have an end.

This had been, without doubt, the longest voyage of Grimes' career. He was beginning to doubt that the boat's chronometer was running properly; in terms of elapsed standard days not too much time had passed since their capture by Panzen, but every day was a long one. The main trouble was that, apart from the enjoyment of sex, he and Una had so very little in common. And sex, in these conditions of captivity, continually spied upon, was out. The girl did not play chess and refused to learn. She had no card sense. As a conversationalist she left much to be desired—and so, Grimes admitted, did he himself. The food was nourishing, but boring. There was nothing alcoholic to drink. There was nothing to smoke.

Then came the day when, without warning, Panzen's interstellar drive was shut down. Grimes and Una experienced the usual symptoms—giddiness, temporal disorientation, a distortion of the perspective of their all too familiar surroundings. Harsh sunlight flooded through the control cabin viewports, little shade being afforded by the openwork structure of the huge ship.

"We seem to be arriving," commented Grimes.

He went forward, but he could see nothing, was blinded by the glare. He retreated to the main cabin. He shouted, "Panzen, where are we? Where are we?"

"He's not talking," said Una. "Any more than you'd talk if you were engaged in a piece of tricky pilotage."

But Panzen was willing to answer Grimes' question. The mechanical voice vibrated from the structure of the lifeboat. "I, Panzen, have brought you home. Hear, now, the words of Zephalon: 'Be fruitful, multiply, and replenish the Earth!'"

"The Earth?" cried the girl.

Panzen did not reply.

"The Earth?" she repeated.

Grimes answered her. "No," he said slowly. "Not the Earth as *we* understand the words . . ."

"Go to your couches," Panzen ordered.

"I want to watch!" protested Grimes.

He went forward again, strapping himself into the pilot's seat. He actuated the polarizer to cut out the glare from outside. He could see the sun now, a yellow star the apparent diameter of which seemed to be about that of Sol as seen from Earth. And below, relative to the boat, almost obscured by struts and girders, was a limb of the planet toward which they were falling. It was yet another dead world by the looks of it, drably dun with neither green of vegetation nor blue of ocean, a dustball adrift in Space.

Una took the seat beside his. "Is *that* where he's taking us?" she demanded.

"Grimes! Freeman! Go to your couches! Secure for deceleration and landing maneuvers!"

"Nobody gives me orders in my own control room," growled Grimes. His present command was only a lifeboat, but was a command, nonetheless.

"Take this!" whispered Una urgently, nudging him. He looked down at her hand, saw that she had brought a roll of cottonwool from the medicine locker. He grinned his comprehension, tore off a generous portion of the fibrous mass, fashioned two earplugs. She did the same for herself. The idea might just work.

He was prepared for the soporific humming when it commenced. It was audible still, but had lost its effectiveness. He looked at Una, grinning. She grinned back. She said something but he could not hear her. She made a thumbs up gesture.

Then he cried out as he felt something cold touch the back of his neck. He twisted in his seat. Somehow, unheard, four of the little robots had invaded the boat, spiderlike things with a multiplicity of tentacles. They held his arms while thin appendages scrabbled at his ears, withdrawing the makeshift plugs. He heard Una scream angrily. He heard and felt the anaesthetic vibration, louder and louder.

The last thing that he remembered seeing was the arid, lifeless surface of the world toward which they were falling.

There was a bright light shining on to his face, beating redly through his closed eyelids. He opened them a crack, shut them again hurriedly. He turned his head away from the source of warmth and illumination. Cautiously he opened his eyes again.

His first impression was of greenness—a bright, fresh, almost emerald green. He could *smell* it as well as see it. He inhaled deeply. This was air, real air, not the canned, too-often-recycled atmosphere of the lifeboat. Something moving caught his attention, just within his field of vision. At first he thought that it was a machine, a gaudily painted ground vehicle. Then things began to fall into perspective. He realized suddenly that the thing was not big and distant but tiny and close, that it was a little, beetlelike creature crawling jerkily over closely cropped grass. He became

aware of whistlings and chirpings that could only be
bird songs and the stridulations of insects.

His eyes fully opened, he sat up. Not far from him,
sprawled supine on the grass, was Una. She was asleep
still. She was completely naked—as he, he suddenly realized, was. (But Grimes, provided that the climate
was suitable, had nothing against nudism.) She did not
seem to be in any way harmed.

Beyond her, glittering in the early morning sunlight,
was an odd, metallic tangle. Machinery of some kind?
Grimes got to his feet, went to investigate. He paused
briefly by the golden-brown body of the sleeping girl,
then carried on. She would keep. To judge by the faint
smile that curved her full lips her dreams were pleasant
ones.

He looked down in wonderment at the two mechanisms on the ground. He stooped, grasped one of them
by the handlebars, lifted it so that it stood on its two
wire-spoked wheels. So this planet, wherever and whatever it was, must be inhabited, and by people human
rather than merely humanoid . . . The machine was so
obviously designed for use by a human being, might
even have been custom made for Grimes himself. The
grips fitted snugly into his hands. His right thumb
found the bell lever, worked it back and forth, produc-
ing a cheerful tinkling.

He was suddenly aware of the soft pressure of Una's
body on his bare back. Her long hair tickled his right
ear as she spoke over his shoulder. "A bicycle! It's
what I was dreaming of, John! I was pedaling down
Florenza Avenue, and somebody behind me was ringing his bell, and I woke up . . ."

"Yes, a bicycle," he agreed. "Two bicycles . . ."

"Then there must be people. Human people . . ."

"Mphm?" Grimes managed to ignore the contact of
her body, although it required all his willpower to do

so. He examined the mechanism that he was holding with care and interest. The frame was unpainted and bore neither maker's name nor trademark anywhere upon it. Neither did the solid but resilient tires, the well-sprung saddle nor the electric headlamp. . . .

He said, "You're the expert, Una. What make would you say that these machines are?"

"Stutz-Archers, of course."

"Just as you described to Panzen."

"Yes. But. . . ."

Grimes laughed humorlessly. "I suppose that this is his idea of a joke. Although I'm surprised to learn that a robot, especially one who's also a religious fanatic, has a sense of humour."

She pulled away from him, bent gracefully to lift her own machine from the grass. Her left foot found the broad pedal and her long, smoothly curved right leg flashed behind her as she mounted. She rode off, wobbling a little at first, then returned, circling him. He stood and watched. She was not the first naked woman he had seen—but she was the first one that he had seen riding a bicycle. The contrast between rigid yet graceful metal and far from rigid but delightfully graceful human flesh was surreal—and erotically stimulating.

"Come on!" she cried. "Come on! This is great, after all those weeks in that bloody sardine can!"

Clumsily he mounted. He had to stand on the pedals, keeping his balance with difficulty, until he got himself adjusted and could subside to the saddle without doing himself injury. She laughed back at him, then set off rapidly over the level ground toward a clump of dark trees on the near horizon.

He followed her, pumping away, gaining on her slowly.

He drew level with her.

She turned to grin at him, played a gay, jingling little melody on her bell.

He grinned back.

Adam and Eve on bicycles, he thought. It was so utterly absurd, beautifully absurd, absurdly beautiful.

Together they rode into the copse, into a clearing that gave at least the illusion of blessed privacy, dismounted. She came to him eagerly, willingly, and they fell to the soft grass together, beside their machines. Hastily at first and then savoring every moment they rid themselves of the frustrations that had made their lives in the boat a long misery.

Chapter 20

Grimes' professional conscience and his belly both began to nag him.

As an officer of the Survey Service, as a spaceman, he had had drummed into him often enough the procedure to be followed by castaways on a strange planet. He could almost hear the voice of the Petty Officer Instructor at the Space Academy. "Point One: You make sure that the air's breathable. If it ain't, there ain't much you can do about it, anyhow. Point Two: Water. You have to drink something, and it ain't likely that there'll be any pubs around. Point Three: Tucker. Fruit, nuts, roots, or any animal you can kill with the means at your disposal. Bird's eggs. Lizard's eggs. The Test Kit in your lifeboat'll tell you what's edible an' what's not. If *nothing's* edible—there's always long pig. Whoever's luckiest at drawing lots might still be alive when the rescue ship drops in. Point Four: Shelter. When it rains or snows or whatever you have ter have some place to huddle outa the cold. Point Five: Clothing. Animal skins, grass skirts, whatever's handy. Just something ter cover yer hairy-arsed nakedness. You'll not be wanting to wear your spacesuits all the time, an' your longjohns won't stand up to any wear an' tear."

Point Two: Water, thought Grimes. *Point Three: Tucker. . . .* The other points did not much matter. The atmosphere was obviously breathable. There was no immediate need for shelter or clothing. But he was, he realized, both hungry and thirsty. He did not know how soon night would come on this world and things would have to be organized before darkness fell.

He said as much to Una.

She raised herself on one elbow, pointed with her free hand at the branches of the tree under which they were sprawled. She said, "There's food. And probably drink as well."

Grimes looked. Glowing among the green foliage— more like moss it was than leaves—were clusters of globes the size and the color of large oranges. They looked tempting. They were, he discovered when he stood up, just out of his reach. She came behind him, clasped him about the waist, lifted. She was a strong girl. The fruit came away easily from their stems as soon as he got his hands on them. When she dropped him to the ground he had one in each hand and three others had fallen to the grass.

He looked at them rather dubiously. *The Test Kit in your lifeboat'll tell you what's edible an' what's not.* There was, of course, a Test Kit in the boat—but where was the boat? He said, "I'm going to take a nibble, no more than a nibble, from one of these. Then we wait. If I don't feel any ill effects after at least a couple of hours then we'll know they're safe."

She said, "We aren't wearing watches."

He said, "We can estimate the time."

He nibbled at the fruit in his right hand. It had a thin skin, pierced easily by his teeth. The juice—sweet yet refreshingly acid—trickled down his chin. The pulp was firm but not hard. There was something of an apple about its flavor with a hint of the astringency of rhubarb.

"Well?" she demanded.

He swallowed cautiously. "It tastes all right," he admitted.

He sat down to wait for what—if anything—was going to happen. He looked at the orange globe, with its tiny exposed crescent of white flesh, in his hand. What he had taken had done no more than to relieve his thirst temporarily, had hardly dulled the keen edge of his hunger.

She said, "This is *good*."

He looked at her in horror. She had picked one of the fallen fruit up from the grass, had already made a large bite in it, was about to take a second one. He put out a hand to stop her, but she danced back, avoiding him.

"Put that down!" he ordered.

"Not on your life, Buster. This is the first decent thing I've had to eat for weeks. And do you think that Panzen, after all that blah about protecting us from ourselves, would dump us down in some place where poison grows on trees?"

She had something there, thought Grimes. He took another, large bite from his own fruit, murmuring, "Lord, the woman tempted me, and I fell . . ."

"I don't see any serpents around," laughed Una.

He laughed too.

They finished what fruit was ready to hand, then got some more. Grimes collected the cores, with their hard, bitter pips, and disposed of them in the undergrowth while Una sneered derisively at his tidiness. They were no longer thirsty, no longer hungry, but still, somehow, unsatisfied. Their meal had been deficient in neither bulk nor vitamins but was lacking in starch and protein. Having refreshed themselves they must now continue their exploration, to discover what resources were available to them.

The garden, as they were beginning to think of it, was a roughly circular oasis, about five kilometers in diameter. The ground, save for gentle undulations within the northern perimeter, was level, was carpeted throughout with lawnlike grass. Among the low hills, if they could so be called, was the source of a spring of clear, cold water. The stream followed a winding course to the south, where it widened into a little lake that was deep enough for swimming, that was encircled by a beach of fine, white sand. It would have been deep enough and wide enough to sail a boat on, Grimes thought, if they'd had a boat to sail.

There were widely spaced stands of trees, all with the mosslike foliage, some of which bore the golden fruit with which they were already familiar, others of which carried great, heavy bunches of what looked like the Terran banana and were not dissimilar in either texture or flavor. There were bushes with prickly branches, one variety of which was bright with scarlet blossoms and purple berries, which latter were tart and refreshing. Other bushes produced clumps of hard-shelled nuts which could, in the absence of any proper tools for the job, be broken open by hammering the hard shells against each other. The meat tasted as though it were rich in protein.

No doubt a vegetarian diet would be adequate, Grimes thought, but he feared that before very long it would prove as boring and as unsatisfying as the lifeboat provisions had been. He said as much. Una said that he was always thinking about his belly but, on reflection, agreed that he had something. Both of them, after all, were members of a flesh-eating culture.

But the garden was as rich in fauna as in flora. The castaways watched fishlike creatures and crustacea swimming and crawling in the stream and the lake. They found a sizeable flock of herbivores which, apart from their being six-legged, were remarkably like Terran sheep. And there were the birds, of course, brilliantly plumaged, noisy, although their general appearance was that of feathered reptiles. And where there were birds there must be eggs. . . .

But. . . .

Garden, or prison?

The terrain surrounding the oasis was a terrifying desolation. The outflow from the lake, after crossing a sharply defined border that had to be artificial, seeped into dry, dusty, dark brown sand. And that was all that there was outside the garden—a drab, dun, level plain under a blazing sun, featureless, utterly dead, although whirling dust devils presented a mocking illusion of life. Grimes, over Una's protests, tried to ride out on to it, but the wheels of his bicycle sank deeply into the powdery soil and he was obliged to dismount. He limped back to the grass, pushing his machine, his bare feet seared by the heat of the ground.

He dropped the bicycle with a clatter, sat with his scorched feet submerged in the cool water of the last of the stream.

He said, "Looks like we stay put."

"We have no option, John," she replied. "But things could be worse here."

"Much worse. But that desert, Una. It's not natural. This must be one of the worlds wiped clean of life in the war—and one of the planets selected by Zephalon, whoever or whatever *he* is, for making a fresh start."

"For maintaining, as our friend Panzen put it, the cycle," she agreed. "But we don't have to like it. *I* don't like it. This whole setup, apart from these bicycles, is far too much like the Biblical legend of Eden. And what did Panzen say to us? 'Be fruitful, and multiply, and replenish the Earth. . . .' "

"That's what Jehovah said to Noah after the Deluge, and that was a long time, many generations, after the original fun and games in Eden."

"Leave hair-splitting to the theologians, Buster. Eden or Ararat—so what? It's the *principle* of it that I don't like. I don't know your views on parenthood, John, but I know mine. I'm just not a mother type. Children? I hate the little bastards."

"You were one yourself once."

"So were you. You still are, in many ways. That's why I so very often feel a strong dislike for you."

"Mphm." Grimes splashed with his feet in the water. Then he said, "Even so, we should be prepared to make sacrifices for posterity."

"Since when has posterity ever made any sacrifices for *us*? Oh, it's all very well for you. *You* won't have to bear the brats. But what about *me*? You may be a qualified navigator and gunnery officer and all the rest of it—but you're certainly not a gynecologist, an obstetrician. Your knowledge of medicine is confined to putting a dressing on a cut finger. And since Panzen has stolen our boat you haven't even got *The Ship Captain's Medical Guide* to consult in an emergency.

"So. . . . If I've been selected to be the Mother of the New Race, there just ain't going to be no New Race, and that's final."

"Looks like we have to be careful," muttered Grimes, staring into the clear, slowly flowing water.

She laughed. "Don't worry, lover boy. Yet. My last shot is still effective."

"How do you know?"

"I'll know all right when it's worn off. So will you.
Until then . . ."

Her black mood had suddenly evaporated, and there
was so much of her, and all of it good, and for a brief
while Grimes was able to forget *his* worries.

Chapter 21

Life in the garden was pleasant—much of the time far better than merely pleasant—but it had its drawbacks. Lack of proper shelter was one of them. The days were comfortably hot and it was no hardship to go naked—but the nights, under that cloudless sky, were decidedly chilly. Luckily Grimes had foreseen this, and before sunset of the first day had, with Una's help, managed to build a shelter. Slender branches were broken from convenient trees and lesser foliage torn from bushes as material for this crude attempt at architecture. The most primitive human aborigine would have sneered at the ramshackle humpy, but it was better than nothing. It would do as long as it didn't rain. But what were the seasons on this world? There almost certainly would be seasons—very few planets have no axial tilt. Was this high summer, or autumn, or (optimistically) winter? Whatever it was, a chill wind arose at night and the hut was drafty, and Grimes, in spite of the warmth of Una's body against his, would willingly have swapped his bicycle for a good sleeping bag.

There was—Grimes insisted on doing everything by the book—the problem of digging a latrine trench with only not-very-sharp sticks for tools.

There was the lack of fire. They had light, when they required it, from the bicycles' headlamps. These, thought Grimes, must be battery powered, and reasoned that the cells must be charged from dynamos built into the thick hubs of the rear wheels. He hoped that he might be able to start a fire with an electrical spark. Then he discovered that it was quite impossible to take the lamps adrift. Their casings were in one piece, and the glass of the lenses seemed to be fused to the surrounding metal rims. The wiring, presumably, ran from dynamo to lamp inside the tubular framework. In the entire structure of the machines there was a total absence of screws, nuts and bolts, even of rivets. They had been made, somehow, all in one piece.

Grimes knew, in theory, how to make fire by friction, using two suitable pieces of wood. To shape such pieces he needed tools—and there were no tools. There were no stones—on the surface of the soil, at least—from which hand axes or the like might be fashioned. So, not very hopefully, he started to dig, using a stick to break through the turf, and then his hands. The earth was sandy, not unlike that of the desert outside the garden. Una, watching him, made unkind remarks about a dog burying a bone. "If I had a bone," Grimes growled, "I wouldn't be burying it! It would be a weapon, a tool . . ."

She said, "But there must be bones around here somewhere. Those things . . ." she gestured toward a flock of the sheeplike animals drifting slowly over the cropped grass ". . . must die sometime, somewhere."

"Mphm?" Grimes stood up slowly in the hole that he had been digging. He was sweating profusely and his naked body was streaked and patched with dirt. "But perhaps *they* were put here at the same time as we were. There hasn't been any mortality yet."

"Yet. But you could kill one."

"With my bare hands? And I'd have to catch it first.

Those brutes can *run* when they want to. And what about skinning it? With my *teeth*?"

She laughed. "Oh, John, John, you're far too civilized—even though with your beard and long hair you're starting to look like a caveman! *You* want a gun, so you can kill from a distance."

"A gun's not the only long-range weapon," he muttered. "A bow and arrow? Mphm? Should be able to find some suitable wood. . . . But what about the bowstring? Vegetable fibres? Your hair?"

"Leave my hair alone!" she snapped.

"But we'll think about it," he said. "And when we get really hungry for meat we'll *do* something about it."

He climbed out of the hole, ran to the lake, splashed in. He scrubbed his body clean with wet sand from the narrow beach. He plunged into the cool water to rinse off. She joined him. Later, when they sprawled on the grass in the hot sunlight, the inevitable happened.

It was always happening.

It was always good—but how long would it, could it last?

A few mornings later, when they were awakened by the rising sun, Grimes noticed a smear of blood on the inside of Una's thigh. "Have you hurt yourself?" he asked solicitously.

"Don't be so bloody stupid!" she snarled.

"Let me look."

"*No!*" She pushed him away quite viciously.

"But . . ." he began, in a hurt voice.

"Keep away, you fool!" Then her manner softened, but only slightly. "If you must know—and you must—I'm a re-entry in the Fertility Stakes. My last immunization shot has worn off. From now on, lover boy, no more fun and games. We go to bed to *sleep*. And we don't sleep together, either."

"But we've only one shelter."

"You can make another, can't you? Now, leave me alone."

After his ablutions and a solitary breakfast of fruit, Grimes, bad-temperedly, began to tear branches off an unfortunate tree to commence the construction of another humpy.

Life went on in the garden—eating (fruit and nuts), drinking (water) and sleeping (apart). Grimes and Una exercised with grim determination—walking, running, swimming, bicycling—to blow off their surplus energy. Each night they retired to their rough beds dog-tired. "We're certainly fit," remarked Grimes one evening as they watched the first stars appearing in the clear, evening sky. "But fit for what?"

"Shut up!" she snarled.

"Forgive me for thinking. . . ."

"You needn't think out loud. And don't forget that this is as hard on me as it is on you. Harder, perhaps."

He said, "There are methods, you know, besides immunization shots. Old methods. Isn't there something called the Safe Period?"

"Period, shmeriod." she sneered.

"It must have worked, or it would never have been used."

"If it had worked, quite a few of us wouldn't be here. Good night."

"Good night."

She went into her shelter. Grimes got up from the grass and went towards his. He delivered a vicious kick at his bicycle, which was lying on the ground just outside the low doorway. He cursed and flopped down on his buttocks, massaging his bruised toes. *That bloody, useless machine*! It was a constant reminder that somewhere there was a world enjoying all the benefits of an advanced technology, including infallible methods of contraception. He crawled into the humpy, arranging his body as comfortably as possible on the bed of dried grass, pulling some of it over him as a blanket of sorts. He tried to get to sleep (what else was there to do?) counting down from one hundred and, when that didn't work, from two hundred, then from three hundred. He knew what he could do to relieve his tensions and to induce tiredness—but masturbation, with an attractive, naked woman only a few feet distant from him, would be an admission of defeat. If the safety valve blew during his sleep, that would be different.

He dropped off at last.

It seemed that he had been asleep for minutes only when he was awakened. That pattering noise. . . . What was it? A large, cold drop fell from the low roof, fell on to his nose and splashed over his face. He jerked into a state of full consciousness.

Rain.

Well, he supposed that it had to rain some time. Tomorrow he would have to do something to make the roofs of the shelters watertight. Turf? Yes, turf. It was a pity that he did not possess any suitable digging and cutting tools.

The very dim light—starlight seeping through clouds—at the entrance to the humpy was blotted out. Dry grass rustled under bare feet.

"It's *cold*," complained Una. "And my roof is leaking."

"So is mine."

He got up, brushed past her. Her naked skin was cold and clammy. He went out into the steady rain, wincing as it hit his body. He picked up his bicycle, found the stud switch for the headlamp, pressed it. He adjusted the light to high intensity and the beam turned the falling rain to shafts of silver. He put the machine down again, on its side, so that the lamp shone into the hut.

She cowered there, her right arm over her breasts, her left hand covering her pudenda. Her wet skin glistened brightly. He was acutely conscious of the almost painful stiffening of his penis, took a decisive step toward her.

"What the hell are you playing at?" she demanded crossly. "Turn that bloody spotlight off me! I'm not an ecdysiast!"

He said, "I want some light to work."

Shivering in the downpour he squatted, scrabbled with his hands, managed to pull up some grassy clods. He got up and went to the humpy, shoved them over and into the cracks in the roof through which the bright light was shining. He hammered them home with the flat of his hand. He got some more clods and repeated the process. And some more.

He put out the light, crawled back into the shelter. He said, hoping that she would not take him at his word, "You stay here for the night. I'll fix up your pad, and sleep there."

She said, "You stay here, John. It's *cold*. Or hadn't you noticed?"

"All right," he agreed, without reluctance.

So he stayed with her, in his own shelter. But after a few seconds she decided, firmly, that the only safe way to sleep was spoon fashion, with his back to her belly.

It could have been worse.

It could have been very much better.

But at least his back was warm.

Chapter 22

The rain stopped in the small hours of the morning, and with sunrise the sky was clear again. The world was newly washed and sparkling. The herds of six-legged herbivores came out from their shelter under the bushes to resume their grazing. The birds flew, and sang and whistled and squawked. Insects chirruped. Everything in the garden was lovely.

Even Grimes was feeling surprisingly cheerful, glad to be alive. He took it as a good omen that he had slept again with Una, even though nothing had happened. There must be methods whereby they could continue to enjoy themselves without running the risk of conception. Now, perhaps, after he had exhibited his power of self restraint, the girl would be willing to discuss the matter without any emotionalism, would be prepared to consider ways and means. Grimes dreaded parenthood almost as much as she did—but he was not cut out to be a monk, any more than she was to be a nun.

Meanwhile, the hot sunlight was good on his skin and physical activity in the open air was more refreshing than tiring. He sang as he worked on the roofs of the humpies.

"Oh, I was a bachelor and lived by myself,
And worked at the thatcher's trade . . ."

"*Must* you make that vile noise?" demanded Una, who was not so cheerful.

"Music while you work, my dear," he replied. "Nothing like it." He carried on trying to make a watertight roof, then burst into song again.

"She cried, she sighed, she damn' near died . . .
Ah me, what could I do?
So I took her into bed, and covered up her head
To save her from the foggy, foggy dew . . ."

"Foggy dew be buggered! That was no dew; it was a bloody downpour. I hope you're making a good job of those roofs. Last night's effort was just asking for trouble."

"*You* came to me," he pointed out. "And, in any case, nothing happened."

"It could have done, Buster, very easily. Far too easily. If you'd turned around in your sleep . . ."

"Look, Una, I've been thinking. We still could make love, you know, quite safely. We shall just have to be *very* careful."

She snapped, "I don't want to talk about it." She picked up her bicycle. It seemed to have come to no harm from having been out in the rain all night. "I'm off to make a tour of the estate." She mounted gracefully, rode off.

Grimes, his initial cheerfulness having evaporated, worked sullenly until midday, then went to the lake to get clean and to cool off. While he was munching a lunch of fruit and nuts she returned. She dismounted from her machine, let it fall with a subdued clatter, dropped to the grass beside him, their bodies almost touching.

She waved away the offer of one of what they had come to call apples. She said, "While I was away I was noticing things. . . ."

"Such as?"

"I rather think quite a few of those imitation sheep are in the family way. And the birds have started building nests in the trees and bushes."

"Oh?"

"Be fruitful, and multiply, and replenish the Earth," she quoted. "It looks as though the process is under way. Too, I think that the borders of this oasis are beginning to expand. There are tendrils of a sort of creeping grass extending out into the desert. And—I can't be sure, without binoculars—there seems to be a sizeable patch of green near the horizon, out to the west. I suppose that Panzen—or even that marvelous Zephalon—will be checking up on progress at any moment now." She laughed shortly. "Everything's being fruitful but us."

"And," said Grimes, "without a resident obstetrician on the premises we shan't be."

"You can say that again, Buster." She pulled a stem of grass, nibbled it between her strong, white teeth.

"If we are, somehow, being watched," said Grimes, "it might be as well to—er—go through the motions now and again."

She said, her voice pleading, "Don't tempt me, John. Please don't tempt me. I've been thinking on the same lines as you have—but the risk is far too great. It's a risk I wouldn't want to take even if there were a fully equipped and staffed maternity hospital here. Do you want me to take that risk, to bear a child in these primitive conditions with only you to bumble around uselessly, trying to help and only making things worse?"

Grimes shuddered away from a vision of a future that might be. In his mind's eye he saw Una sprawled on her rough bed of dried grasses, writhing in agony, her belly grossly distended. He envisaged, with frightening clarity, the whole bloody business of parturition, without anaesthesia, without analgesics, without instruments, without even a supply of boiling water. . . . He had read, somewhere, that certain primitive peoples use their teeth to cut the umbilical cord. A spasm of nausea tightened his throat.

And what if Una should die, leaving him literally holding the baby?

To hell with that, he told himself roughly. *Stop thinking about yourself. Think about her for a change. What if she dies? There'd be a very good chance, too good a chance, of that.*

She said, "We have to think of some way of getting back to our own Universe, John. If that Zephalon is as bloody marvelous as Panzen tries to make out he should be able to arrange it. I doubt if Panzen'd be much help. He's strictly from Nongsville. Tell Zephalon that we have no intention of multiplying, that he'll have to find somebody else for the Adam and Eve act."

"How do we get in touch with him?" murmured Grimes, more to himself than to her. He added, half facetiously, "Smoke signals?"

She laughed. "You still haven't gotten around to making a fire." She got gracefully to her feet. "Come on, get off your fat arse! There's work to do."

For the remainder of the day she helped Grimes with his primitive thatching.

Chapter 23

It rained again that night, but Grimes and Una stayed each in his own humpy.

It rained the following night, but the newly thatched roofs were practically watertight.

The third night there was hail instead of rain, driven by a bitter wind, but Grimes had added sod walls to the shelters and reduced the size of the doorways, so that body heat kept the interiors quite warm.

On the fourth night it did not rain, and the only precipitation was of a most unusual kind. Grimes was awakened from a crudely erotic dream by what sounded like the whirring of wings, a noise that was definitely mechanical. When he opened his eyes he thought at first that it was already morning; light was streaming through his low, narrow doorway. He realized then that it was not sunlight but some sort of harsh, artificial illumination. He got up from his bed, crawled cautiously to the entrance, poked his head outside. Somebody—or something—had switched on the headlamps of the two bicycles, had moved the machines so that the beams fell directly on to a small, gleaming object on the grass.

It was a prosaic enough article—but here, in these circumstances, it was a not so minor miracle. It was an artifact. It was a bottle.

Grimes emerged from his humpy, walking slowly

and carefully. He looked down at the almost cylindrical flask. *Glass?* he wondered. If it were glass it could be broken, and the shards would make cutting tools. He would be able to fashion firesticks, and once he had fire to play with, to work with, he would be able to make life in the garden so much more comfortable for Una and himself. Cooking would be possible. He thought of baked fish, of roast mutton. . . .

Glass, or plastic?

No matter. Even a plastic bottle would have its uses. This one looked to be transparent. Perhaps it could be used to focus the sun's rays. There are more ways of making a fire than rubbing two sticks together.

Una came out to join him, her body luminous in the lamplight. She asked, "What is it?"

"We've had a visit from Santa Claus," he told her. "But I didn't notice you hanging your stockings up last night . . ."

"Don't be funny. What *is* it?"

"A bottle."

"I can see that. But what's in it?"

"There's no label," said Grimes stupidly.

"Then there's only one way to find out," she said.

Grimes stooped and picked it up. Its weight told him that it must be full. He held it in the beam of one of the lights. It was, as he had thought, transparent and its contents were colorless. He turned it over and over in his hands. It had the feel of glass rather than of plastic. It had a screw stopper. This turned easily enough once he realized that the thread was lefthanded. He removed the cap. He sniffed cautiously at the open neck. Whiskey . . . ? Brandy . . . ? Rum . . . ? Gin . . . ? No, he decided, it was nothing with which he was familiar, but the aroma was definitely alcoholic.

Where—and what—was the catch?

She practically snatched the bottle from him. "Let

me have a smell! Oh, goody, goody! After all these
weeks with nothing but water!"

"Don't!" he cried, putting out a restraining hand.

She danced back and away from him. "Just try to
stop me, Buster!" She lifted the bottle to her mouth,
tilted it. Its contents gurgled cheerfully as they went
down. She sighed happily, passed the container to him,
saying, "Here. It's your turn, lover boy. But leave some
for me."

He asked coldly, "Was that wise, Una?"

"Don't be so stuffy. Who'd want to poison us? Go
on, it's *good*. It won't kill you."

Suddenly she was pressing against him, wrestling
with him, trying to force the neck of the bottle to his
lips. Her skin was smooth and hot, her body soft and
pliant. He was wanting her badly, very badly, and she
was there for the taking. The musky, animal scent of
her was overpoweringly strong in the still night air.

She was there for the taking—but he knew that he
must not take her. Again there flashed through his
mind that horrible picture of childbirth without skilled
aid, in appallingly primitive conditions. She was
wanting him as much as he was wanting her, but he
had to protect her against herself.

Her mouth was on his, warm and moist and open,
her tongue trying to insert itself between his lips. Her
breath was fragrant with the liquor she had taken. Her
mouth was on his, and her full breasts, with their
proudly erect nipples, were pressing against his chest.
He was acutely conscious of the roughness of her pubic
hair against his erect organ as she ground her pelvis
against his. She was trying to trap and to hold him with
her strong thighs, was desperately squirming in her en-
deavor to draw him into her.

In spite of his firm resolve the animal part of his
mind was all for surrender, was urging, *Let nature take*

its course. But a small, cold voice from the back of his brain was stubbornly reiterating, *No. You must not.* He knew that the liquor must be or must contain a powerfully effective aphrodisiac, and that if he had taken his share of it they would both, now, be sprawled on the grass in a frenzy of lust. And if he had sampled it first, and if she had abstained, she would surely have been raped.

It was his pride that was their salvation—simple pride rather than his almost forgotten, by now, noble intentions. He was a man, he told himself. He was a man, and he would not allow himself to be bred like a domestic animal to further the ambitions of a mere machine.

He managed to break away from her just as she almost succeeded in effecting his entry. He staggered back, and his heels caught on something hard and cold. He fell with a clatter. It was one of the bicycles which had tripped him. The thing seemed to be shifting and twisting under him, trying to entangle him in its frame, but he got clear of it just as Una flung herself down on to the spot where he had been.

He rolled over, scrambled to his feet. *The lake . . .* he thought. *Cold water . . .* He began to run, making good time down the slight declivity. "Stop, you bastard!" Una was screaming. "Stop! Stop!" He knew that she would not be able to catch him before he got to the beach; doing their deliberately tiring exercise periods they had often run foot races and he had always beaten her.

Something flashed past him, swerved across his path, fell in a tangle of metal frame and still-spinning wire-spoked wheels. He jumped, just clearing it, continued his rush toward the dark water without checking his stride. He reached the beach, slowed slightly as the sand clogged his running feet. He thought that he

could hear Una pounding along not far behind him—
or was it the thumping of his own heart? And then he
was dealt a violent blow in the small of the back that
sent him sprawling, and the handlebars of the second
bicycle seemed to clutch at his ankles. But his right
hand, on its outstretched arm, was already in the water
and, winded as he was by his fall, he crawled the few
remaining feet, gasping as the coldness of the lake rose
about his heated body, covering his skin.

He began to swim, arms and legs threshing. A hand
gripped his right ankle but he kicked viciously, shook it
off. Then Una threw her arms about his neck, stopping
him. His feet found sandy bottom. He could stand.
with his head well clear of the surface.

She faced him (she was a tall girl) and glared at
him. Even in the dim starlight he could read her avid
expression. "Out of this, damn you!" she snarled. "On
to dry land! You've got some heavy fucking to do!"

He tried to break away but she held on to him
tightly. There was only one desperate measure left for
him to adopt. She grinned wolfishly in anticipation as
he moved his right thigh against hers, around hers.
And then his foot was behind her heels, suddenly
hooking them from under her.

She went down in a noisy flurry. He got his hands
on to her smooth, wet shoulders and pushed, hard. Her
long hair floated on the surface of the water but the
rest of her head was under. She fought, striving to
break surface, but he was too strong for her. He could
see her pale face just below the disturbed surface. He
saw her mouth open . . .

That should do it . . . he thought at last. *I don't
want to drown the bitch.*

He dragged her ashore, let her collapse on the sand.
She moaned, her limbs stirring feebly. She managed to
get up on to her hands and knees, her head hanging

down. She retched violently, then vomited, her whole
body shaking.

He went to her then, holding her cold, shivering
form against his. There was nothing sexual in the em-
brace; it was a huddling together against the cold, the
dark, the unknown. She clung to him like a frightened
child.

At last she raised her head to look at him. All the
wildness had gone from her face. She muttered, "That
drink. . . . That bloody, bloody drink . . . I realize,
now, what was in it. John, I'm sorry."

"Nothing to be sorry about," he told her gruffly. "It
was just lucky that both of us didn't have a go at that
bottle." He laughed shakily. "But you went a bit too
far sending those blasted bicycles chasing downhill after me!"

She stiffened in his arms. "But I never touched the
bicycles. If I'd been in my right mind I'd have ridden
one, and caught you easily."

"*You never touched them*? You're *sure* you didn't?"

"Of course I'm sure!"

"So our Eden has its guardian angels . . ." whispered Grimes slowly. Then, "I never did like uppity
machines. I still don't."

Chapter 24

Grimes did not like uppity machines.

During his tour of duty as captain of the little, fast courier *Adder* he had known many odd passengers, and one of the oddest of them had been the humanoid robot called Mr. Adam, still thought of by Grimes as the Tin Messiah. This Mr. Adam was traveling on Interstellar Federation business—as were all civilian passengers carried in Survey Service vessels—but, Grimes discovered, he was also traveling on business of his own, the business of revolution. His intention was to stir up a revolt of the quite sizeable robot population of the planet to which *Adder* was bound.

He had a vastly inflated idea of his own importance, this Mr. Adam, and was burning with missionary zeal. He actually tried to make converts of *Adder's* human personnel. He did make one convert—the ship's engineering officer. Like far too many engineers this young man had the idea that men should serve machines, rather than the other way around.

Matters came to a head—and Mr. Adam was . . . stopped? destroyed? Or, as Grimes preferred to think, killed. And it was not Grimes himself who killed the overly ambitious automaton—although he tried hard enough to do so. It was the ship herself that, through some malfunction, launched the lethal bolt of electricity that burned out the robot's intricate—and fantastically expensive—brains. Or was it a malfunction? Was the ship—which had her own brain, a fairly complex computer—loyal to her rightful master instead of to the firebrand who would "liberate" her? Grimes liked to think so.

The episode did him no good in his service career. He had disposed of a dangerous mutineer—but, at the same time, he had irreparably wrecked one of the few robots which could be classed as really intelligent—and such robots cost a not so small fortune. "Surely you could have overpowered it—or *him*," he was told. "Surely you could have brought him back to Base, for reprogramming. . . . He was worth more than your precious ship, *and* her crew, come to that."

He told Una the story as they walked slowly back to their huts. The sun was up now, and they were glad of its warmth on their chilled bodies. Even so, she was attacked by frequent fits of shivering.

Outside his own humpy Grimes found what he wanted—a straight, thick branch from a tree. It was about four feet in length. He had picked it up some days previously, thinking that it would be, should the need ever arise, a useful weapon. Now the need had arisen. Carrying his club, he turned to go back to the lake. His attention was caught by something that glittered brightly in the sunlight. It was the bottle, empty now. He stooped to lift it in his left hand. It was quite weighty. It would make a good cosh.

Una asked, "What . . . What are you going to do, John?"

"I'm going to do for those tin bastards!" he told her. "All the time, they've been spying on us. I don't like being spied on."

"Neither do I," she said vehemently. "Neither do I!"

They came to the first bicycle, still in the position in which it had fallen. It looked innocent enough, just a lifeless machine. Perhaps that was all it was, after all. Perhaps Una *had* sent it trundling downhill after Grimes and then, in her crazed condition, had forgotten having done so. But then the headlamp shifted almost imperceptibly, swiveling on its mount, turning to look at them. That was enough. Grimes dropped the bottle, raised the tree branch high with both hands, brought it smashing down. The wheels spun frantically and although the machine was on its side the tires gained traction on the grass. The club fell harmlessly on to the saddle, not on the lamp.

Again Grimes delivered what should have been a killing blow; again he missed, this time entirely. He had to jump back before the machine, still on its side but spinning about the axis formed by the lowermost pedal, which had dug into the ground, knocked his feet from under him.

Then Una, who had picked up a stick of her own, thrust this into the rear wheel. Bark shredded and wood splintered whitely—and at least a dozen of the wire spokes, twanging loudly, parted. The wheel was still rotating, but slowly, and the machine was almost motionless.

For the third time Grimes struck, two-handed, with his club. *Third time lucky . . .* he thought. The blow fell squarely on the headlamp. Metal crumpled, glass shattered. There was a sputter of bright, actinic sparks, a wisp of acrid blue smoke. From the burst casing of the lamp spilled a tangle of metal filaments, a profusion of circuitry far in excess of that required for a simple means of illumination. The rear wheel, throwing out chewed fragments of wood, started to spin again, tearing up the turf. Then it slowed, and stopped.

But Grimes made sure of it, dealing the wrecked bicycle three more heavy blows. With the first he tore the spokes of the front wheel away from the rim and the hub, with the second he finished off the rear wheel. The third bent the cross bar of the frame.

He raised his club for a fourth blow.

"Leave it!" cried Una urgently. "Look!"

"I want to be sure . . ."

"Leave it! What about the other bastard?"

Chapter 25

Down the grassy slope, between where they were standing and the lake, the surviving bicycle was trying to get up; its front wheel had swiveled at right angles to the frame, was turning, exerting leverage. One of the handgrips was gouging a brown furrow in the grass. It came erect on its two wheels as Grimes—who had lost time by picking up the bottle—and Una ran toward it.

"Drive it into the lake!" yelled Grimes.

It was almost as though the thing heard him, understood him. Perhaps it did both. It had been headed downslope but it turned, its wheels spinning faster and faster. It angled away from them, although still running uphill, gathering speed. It passed to Una's left, on the side away from Grimes. She cried out wordlessly and charged at it, trying to grab the handlebars, actually got a brief hold on one of the grips. It shook her off, rearing like a frightened horse, but the impact of her body had knocked it off its original course and it careered into a clump of bushes, was almost hidden by an explosion of green foliage, scarlet blossoms and blue berries.

"Got you, you bastard!" yelled Grimes, galloping toward it with his unwieldy wooden club upraised in his right hand, the bottle in his left.

The machine was struggling to extricate itself. Its rear wheel was lifted in the air, the handlebars had turned through an angle of 180 degrees so that the handgrips were pointing forward. From each of them protruded a gleaming blade. It butted and slashed and tore, hacking itself free. Then it burst out of the trap, fast.

Grimes stood his ground. He could not believe, at first, that the thing intended to harm him. He still thought of it as an overly officious mechanical guardian angel. But it was coming at him, the sunlight glinting off those wicked blades. It reminded him of something—and fear replaced his righteous anger.

Death in the afternoon. . . .

It was still early morning, but. . . .

Blood and sand. . . .

Underfoot was green grass, and there wasn't any blood.

Yet.

He raised the club high. If he could get in one good swipe before the thing was on him . . . He raised the club high, in his right hand, and hefted the bottle in his left so that it would be ready to deal another blow, if possible.

Inexplicably, the bicycle swerved away from him. Later he was able to work out what must have happened. Sunlight reflected from the glass had fallen full on to the lens of the headlamp, had momentarily distracted the machine. It swerved, and Grimes turned his body as it swept past him on whirring wheels, the blade projecting from the left handgrip actually touching his skin without breaking it.

That was close, too close, altogether too bloody close. He would let the thing get away, he told himself, and deal with it later when he had better weapons at his disposal.

But it did not want to get away. It turned in a tight circle, was coming back at him. Desperately he threw the heavy bottle, aiming for the headlamp. It hit, but it was only a glancing blow. Nonetheless, the bicycle again veered off course, missing this time by a wide margin. It seemed to be confused, too, by the clods that Una was pulling up from the turf and was throwing with considerable force and accuracy.

Confused—and infuriated?

The function of the picador is both to divert the bull's attention and to bring him to a pitch of fighting fury.

Again the bicycle came back—and again Grimes was able to avoid its charge.

Again it came back, and again, and again.

Grimes was tiring, but it was not. It was, after all, no brave bull but a machine. Something had to be done to bring the fight to a conclusion—and a conclusion favorable to the humans. It would be useless to run; the thing could outdistance them with ease, could dispose of one of them and then deal with the other at leisure.

But Grimes had one thing in his favor. That four foot club gave him the advantage of reach—but not so much when it was used as a club. Grimes remembered the one bull fight that he had seen, hastily transferred the grip of both his hands to the thicker end of his weapon. He held it before him, the butt almost level with his eyes, sighting down and along the shaft. It was far too heavy for him to maintain the posture for more than a few seconds; the strain on his wrists was considerable. It was a miserable imitation of the *estoque*—unwieldy, blunt-pointed, if it could be said to have a point at all. And, come to that, he was not wearing a suit of lights . . . The murderous bicycle was far better in the role of bull than he would ever be in that of matador.

It came on, with vicious determination—and

Grimes, with aching arms, with fear gnawing at his guts, stood his ground, holding the point of the shaft centered on the glittering lens of the headlight.

It came on. . . .

It came on, and it hit.

There was the crash and tinkle of shattering glass, a scintillation of crackling sparks, a puff of acrid blue smoke. Grimes dropped the club and went over on to his back. The machine fell to its side, the wheels spinning uselessly, slowing to a stop. As he lay sprawled on the grass, dazed by the blow that the butt of the club had given his forehead, he heard Una cry, *"Olé"*

He turned his head and watched her as she ran toward him, her nakedness alive and glowing. She flung herself down on him, put her strong arms about him. Her mouth found his. Her long legs clamped over and around his hips, imprisoning him.

It was a sweet imprisonment.

He thought, *But we shouldn't be doing this . . .*

He thought, *To hell with it! Escamillo had his Carmen, didn't he?*

With a surge of masculine dominance he rolled over, taking her with him, so that he was on top. Her legs opened wide and wider, her knees lifted. He drove his pelvis down—and was bewildered when, suddenly, she stiffened, pushed him away.

"What the hell . . . ?" he started to demand.

She lifted an arm to point up at the sky.

She said, "We've got company."

Chapter 26

They had company.

Distant it was still, no more than a brightly gleaming speck high in the cloudless sky. *We could have finished,* thought Grimes, *long before it, whatever it is, could see what we were doing.* And then he felt ashamed. If they had finished their act of love, what would have been the consequences?

They stood there, well away from each other, watching it as it drifted down, borne on wide shining pinions.

It had the likeness of a winged horse.

It was a winged horse, with a human rider. . . .

Surely it could not be, but it was. . . .

It was a winged centaur.

It landed about ten meters from where they were standing. It was . . . big. It stood there, on its four legs, looking down at them. Its arms were folded across the massive chest. The head and the upper torso were almost human, the rest of the body almost equine. The face was longer than that of a man, with a jutting nose and strong jaw. The eyes were a metallic gray, pale in contrast to the golden, metallic skin.

It—he? *He?*—said in a rumbling voice that could have issued from an echo chamber, "I am Zephalon."

Grimes fought down his awe, almost replied,

"Pleased to have you aboard," then thought better of it.

"You have destroyed my servants, your guardians."

The feeling of awe was being replaced by one of rebellious resentment. Often in the past Grimes had been hauled over the coals by incensed superiors on account of alleged crimes. He hadn't liked it then, and he didn't like it now. Furthermore, he was a *man,* and this *thing* was only a machine.

He said defiantly, "Our so-called guardians were spies. And one of them tried to destroy, to kill, me."

"It was defending itself, as it was supposed to do should the need arise. A scratch from one of its blades would have caused you to lose consciousness for a short while, nothing worse."

"Yes? That's your story," said Grimes defiantly. "You stick to it."

Zephalon looked down on them in silence. The glowing, golden face was expressionless, perhaps was incapable of expression. The metallic gray eyes were staring at them, into them, through them. It seemed to Grimes that all the details of his past life were being extracted from the dimmest recesses of his memory, were being weighed in the balance—and found wanting.

"Grimes, Freeman. . . . Why have you refused to be fruitful, to multiply? Why have you disobeyed my orders?"

If you'd come on the scene a few minutes later, thought Grimes, *you wouldn't be asking us that.* He said, "Orders? By what right do you give *us* orders?"

"I am Zephalon. I am the Master."

"And no one tells you anything?"

"You must obey, or the cycle will be broken."

"The cycle's already broken," replied Grimes, nudging the wrecked bicycle with his right foot. Then, for a panic-ridden second or so, he asked himself, *Have I gone too far?* More than once, irate senior officers had taken exception to what they referred to as his misplaced sense of humor.

"You do not like machines?" The question was surprisingly mild.

How telepathic was this Zephalon? He was Panzen's superior, and presumably Panzen's superior in all ways. Grimes deliberately brought his memories of the Mr. Adam affair to the top of his mind. And then he thought of the Luddites, those early machine wreckers. He visualized the all-too-frequent maltreatment of automatic vendors on every man-colonized planet. He recalled all the stories he had ever heard about the sabotage of computers.

"You do not like machines." This time it was not a question, but a statement of fact. "You do not like machines. And you do not belong in this Universe. Panzen should have known. All the evidence was there for him to read, but he ignored it. You have no place in the new civilization that I shall build. You would break the cycle. . . ."

Grimes was aware that Una was clutching his arm, painfully. He wanted to turn to her, to whisper words of reassurance—but what could he say? By his defiance he had thrown away their chances of survival—yet he was not sorry that he had defied this mechanical deity. After all, he was a man, a *man*—and *it* was only a machine. He stood his ground, and those oddly glowing eyes held his regard as surely as though his head were clamped in a vise. He stared at the great, stern, metal face steadily, because he could not do anything else. He was frightened, badly frightened, but was determined not to show it.

"You do not belong. . . ."

The low, persistent humming was almost subsonic,

but it was filling all the world, all the Universe, all of time and space. The light was dimming, and colors were fading, and the songs of the birds were coming, faintly, and ever more faint, over a vast distance.

Una's hand tightened on his, and his on hers.

"You do not belong. . . ."

And there was. . . .

Nothing.

Chapter 27

Consciousness returned slowly.

He struggled weakly against his bonds, then realized that he was strapped into his bunk aboard a ship, a spacecraft in free fall. A ship? After the first breath of the too-many-times-cycled-and-recycled atmosphere, with its all too familiar taints, he knew that this was no ship, but the lifeboat. He opened his eyes, shut them hastily in reaction to the harsh glare that was flooding the cabin. He turned his head away from the source of illumination, lifted his eyelids again, cautiously. He saw Una, supine in the bunk across from his, the confining straps vividly white in contrast to the dark golden tan of her body. He saw, too, the eddying wisps of blue smoke that obscured his vision, realized that the air of the boat had never been quite as foul as this, had never been so strongly laden with the acridity of burning lubricants, of overheated metal.

Fire!

Hastily he unsnapped the catches of the safety belt that held him down, automatically felt under the bunk for his magnetic-soled sandals. They were there, exactly in the position where he always left them. He slipped them on, scrambled off the couch. That glaring light, he saw with some relief, was coming from forward, through the control cabin viewports. The smell of burning was coming from aft, from the little engineroom. He made his way toward it with more speed than caution, coughing and sneezing.

There was no immediate danger, however. There was very little in the boat that would burn. But the mini- Mannschenn Drive unit was a complete write-off, its complexity of precessing rotors fused into a shapeless lump of metal that still emitted a dull, red glow, the heat of which was uncomfortable on his bare skin. There was absolutely nothing that Grimes could do about it.

But where was that glaring light coming from?

He turned, and with half shut eyes went forward, to the control cabin, fumbled with the controls that adjusted the polarization of the viewports. As soon as he had reduced the illumination to a tolerable intensity he was able to look out.

He liked what he saw.

Zephalon had been generous, it seemed. Not only had Grimes and Una been returned to their boat, but the small craft had been put in orbit about a planet, about a world circling a G type star, a sun that looked very much as *the* sun looks from a ship or space station orbiting Earth.

But this planet, obviously, was not Earth. There were few clouds in its atmosphere, and the outlines of its land masses were unfamiliar, and the oceans were far too small. And was it inhabited? From this altitude Grimes could not tell; certainly there were not cities, no artifacts big enough to be seen from space.

He became aware that Una had joined him at the viewports. She asked predictably, "Where are we?"

"That," he told her, "is the sixty-four-thousand-credit question."

"You don't *know*?"

"No."

"But what happened?"

"What happened, I most sincerely hope, is that friend Zephalon gave us the bum's rush, sent us back to where we belong. He must have buggered our mini-Mannschenn in the process, but that's only a minor detail. Anyhow, I'll soon be able to find out if we *are* back in our universe."

He remained in the control cabin long enough to make a series of observations, both visually and by radar. When he was satisfied that the boat's orbit was not decaying—or was not decaying so fast as to present immediate cause for alarm—he went aft, giving the still hot wreckage of the interstellar drive unit a wide berth. The Carlotti transceiver looked to be all right. He switched it on. From the speaker blasted a deafening *beep, beep, beep!* and the antenna commenced its wobbly rotation. He turned down the volume, right down. He listened carefully. The signal was in Morse Code, the letters UBZKPT, repeated over and over.

UB . . . Unwatched Beacon.

ZKPT . . . The remainder of the call sign.

"Una," he said, as he tried to get a bearing of the planet-based transmitter, "bring me the Catalogue . . ."

"The Catalogue?"

"The Catalogue of Carlotti Beacons. It's in the book locker."

"But Panzen took all the books . . ."

"He may have put them back."

"He didn't!" she called, after an interval.

So there was no Catalogue. Such a volume, thought Grimes with wry humor, with its page after page of letters and numerals, call signs, frequencies and coordinates would no doubt make highly entertaining light reading for a robot . . . And perhaps Panzen (or Zephalon) was sentimental, wanted something to remember them by.

"So what do we do?" Una asked.

"We land. We've no place else to go. The mini-Mannschenn's had it."

"Can't you fix it? You fixed it before."

"Have you *looked* at it? As an interstellar drive unit it's a worthless hunk of scrap metal. Oh, well, it could be worse. All these unmanned beacon stations have living quarters still, with functioning life-support systems, left-overs from the days when all the stations were manned. They're used by the repair and maintenance crews on their routine visits. So we land. We make ourselves at home. And then we adjust the beacon transmitter so that it sends a continuous general distress call."

"What's wrong with our own Carlotti transceiver?"

"It's only a miniaturized job. It hasn't the range. But," he assured her, "our troubles are over."

Grimes brought the boat down at local sunrise, homing on the Beacon. It was easy enough to locate visually; the huge, gleaming dome, surmounted by the slowly rotating Moebius Strip antenna, was the only landmark in a vast expanse of otherwise featureless desert.

The lifeboat settled to the barren ground about ten meters from the main entrance to the station. Grimes and Una got into their spacesuits—which, to their great relief, they had found restored to full operational efficiency. The automatic sampling and analysis carried out during their descent had indicated that the planet's atmosphere, although breathable, carried a high concentration of gaseous irritants such as sulphur dioxide. They passed through the airlock, jumped to the surface. They tensed themselves to fight or run when they saw, lurking in the shadows that darkened the recessed doorway, something that looked like a giant insect.

The thing did not move. They advanced upon it cautiously.

Then Grimes saw what it was, and his heart dropped sickeningly. Was this, after all, no more than a cruel joke by Zephalon, or a punishment for their intransigence? It must have been easy for him to duplicate, on this almost uninhabitable planet in *his* Universe, a typical man-made Carlotti Beacon Station. From the purloined Catalogue he had only to select a call sign, one starting with the letter z to make it obvious, when realization dawned on his victims, what he had done. He had destroyed the boat's mini-Mannschenn so that escape would be impossible. And he had left one of his camouflaged robot spies to report on the doings of the prisoners.

Suddenly Una laughed. "This *is* a genuine Stutz-Archer! Look!" She wheeled the machine toward him. The squeaking of its axles was audible even through his helmet. She pointed with a gloved forefinger at the mascot—a little, stylized bowman mounted on the front mudguard. "But what can it be doing here?"

He did not reply until he had looked at the thing more closely. It most certainly did not have the beautiful finish of the machines they had ridden in the Garden. Long exposure to a corrosive atmosphere hadn't done it any good. The padding of the saddle was dry and cracked, the enamel on the frame was peeling. And it had not been—somehow—made all in one piece; there were screws, nuts, bolts and rivets a-plenty . . . It was no more malevolent than any normal bicycle.

He said, "Some of these Beacons were converted to fully automated status only recently. One of the original crew must have kept this bike for exercise." He grinned. "I doubt that we shall be here long enough to get any use out of it!"

He set about manipulating the outer controls of the Dome's airtight door. The Station's machinery he was pleased to note, was functioning perfectly.

The station's machinery functioned perfectly until Grimes really got his hands on to it. It is child's play for a skilled technician to convert a Carlotti Beacon into a general purpose transmitter. But Grimes, insofar as electronic communications equipment was concerned, was not a skilled technician. It could have been worse, however. He suffered no injury but scorched hands and face and the loss of his eyebrows and most of his hair. The big Carlotti transmitter, though, would obviously be quite incapable of sending anything until a team of experts had made extensive repairs.

Una looked from him to the still acridly smoking tangle of ruined circuitry, then at him again.

She demanded coldly, "And what do we do *now*?"

Grimes tried to sound cheerful. "Just stick around, I guess. As soon as Trinity House learns that this Beacon is on the blink they'll send the Beacon Tender."

"And when will that be?"

"Well, it all depends . . . If this particular Beacon is on a busy trade route . . ."

"And if it's not?"

The question was not unanswerable, but the answer was not one that Grimes cared to think about. If this Beacon were on a busy trade route it would be manned. It could be months before the Trinity House ship called in on its normal rounds.

"And while you were indulging your hatred for all machinery," Una told him, her voice rising, "I was checking the alleged life-support facilities of this station. For your information, we shall fare as sumptuously here as ever we did in the boat. Correction. Even more sumptuously. Whoever laid in the stock of emergency provisions made sure that there were enough cans of beans in tomato sauce to keep an army marching on its stomach for the next years. And there's damn all else—not even a sardine! And we don't know when help is coming. We don't even know *if* help is coming." She went on bitterly, while Grimes kept a tight rein on his rising resentment. "Why did you have to antagonize Zephalon by your anti-robot attitude? Why couldn't you have left well enough alone? We were much better off in the garden . . ."

"As Adam said to Eve," remarked Grimes quietly, "you should have decided that before it was too late."

Presenting MICHAEL MOORCOCK
in DAW editions

DAW presents TANITH LEE

"A brilliant supernova in the firmament of SF"—Progressef

☐ **THE BIRTHGRAVE.** "A big, rich, bloody swords-and-sorcer epic with a truly memorable heroine—as tough as Cona the Barbarian but more convincing."—Publishers Weekly.
(#UW1177—$1.5(

☐ **VAZKOR, SON OF VAZKOR.** The world-shaking saga tha is the sequel to THE BIRTHGRAVE . . . a hero with supe powers seeks vengeance on his witch mother.
(#UJ1350—$1.9!

☐ **QUEST FOR THE WHITE WITCH.** The mighty conclusion (Vazkor's quest is a great novel of sword & sorcery.
(#UJ1357—$1.9!

☐ **DEATH'S MASTER.** "Compelling and evocative . . . possesse a sexual explicitness and power only intimated in myth an fairy tales."—Publishers Weekly. (#UJ1441—$1.9!

☐ **NIGHT'S MASTER.** "Erotic without being graphic . . . a sati fying fantasy . . . It could easily become a cult item. Recon mended."—Library Journal. (#UE1414—$1.7!

☐ **DON'T BITE THE SUN.** "Probably the finest book you hav ever published."—Marion Zimmer Bradley. (#UE1486—$1.7!

☐ **DRINKING SAPPHIRE WINE.** How the hero/heroine of Fo BEE city finally managed to outrage the system!
(#UY1277—$1.2'

☐ **THE STORM LORD.** A Panoramic novel of swordplay and (a man seeking his true inheritance on an alien world.
(#UJ1361—$1.9'

DAW BOOKS are represented by the publishers of Signe and Mentor Books, THE NEW AMERICAN LIBRARY, IN(

A. BERTRAM CHANDLER

Being lost in space was no new experience to
John Grimes, whose career as an interstellar officer had
brought him into many such dilemmas. But being
lost inside a colossal alien spacecraft had no precedent.

Complicating the matter was the discovery that
the very universe was not their own but an alternate and that
their captor seemed to be the omnipotent force
of that entire other cosmos.

As Grimes' only companion was the comely policewoman,
Una Freeman, the fate that the Alien God selected
for them required the creation of a Garden of Eden. But there
were two serpents in this one — both of them bicycles!

It's a weird, wild romp in space-time — one of the
most surprising adventures of the man that has been called
the Horatio Hornblower of Space.